THE BEST DEFENSE . . .

We stepped into the alley and began walking in the direction of the car. We were close to the end when two figures came around the corner and started toward us.

I took Jamie's arm and spun her around. As I did, three more figures came out of the door of the restaurant and cut us off. I pushed Jamie against the wall but she squirmed out from behind me. She bent down and picked up a small piece of wood. I had my cane.

"Maybe they just want to talk," she said.
"Maybe they're after my autograph."
"Hunter," she said, "I've never done this before."
"This is one helluva time to bring it up."

A Russian accented voice asked, "The ikon, where is it?"

I lashed out with the cane and smashed him in the middle of the face. So much for detente.

Other Avon Books by
Eric Sauter

HUNTER

Coming Soon

HUNTER AND RAVEN

HUNTER
AND THE IKON

ERIC SAUTER

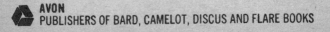
AVON
PUBLISHERS OF BARD, CAMELOT, DISCUS AND FLARE BOOKS

HUNTER AND THE IKON is an original publication of
Avon Books. This work has never before appeared in book
form.

AVON BOOKS
A division of
The Hearst Corporation
1790 Broadway
New York, New York 10019

Copyright © 1984 by Eric Sauter
Published by arrangement with the author
Library of Congress Catalog Card Number: 83-91187
ISBN: 0-380-86546-7

First Avon Printing, February 1984

AVON TRADEMARK REG. U. S. PAT. OFF. AND IN
OTHER COUNTRIES, MARCA REGISTRADA, HECHO EN
U. S. A.

Printed in the U. S. A.

WFH 10 9 8 7 6 5 4 3 2 1

FOR BETH

AUTHOR'S NOTE:

I want to thank Andy Goidich for his help with the religious aspects of this book.

1

OUTSIDE, through the steamed-up windows of the greenhouse, the river was a perfect white landscape of snow-encrusted ice. It was January and the snow had drifted ass-high to a tall Indian, my father's favorite winter phrase, worth repeating exactly once. I wiped off some of the condensation, and saw a nervous-looking squirrel getting into a serious discussion with a bunch of ratty starlings. I wanted the squirrel to win. Two of the birds dive-bombed his little gray head, and he scurried frantically for the safety of a nearby tree. I returned to my coffee and newspaper with a sigh.

"What was that for?" Jamie asked, holding up her perfectly pink grapefruit.

"The squirrel," I said.

"He chicken out again?" She said, squeezing the last bit of juice into the spoon. She reached under the table and scratched Jules on the back of her head. Jules is my dog and likes to be included in the conversation.

"Did anyone tell you that you have a sharp tongue early in the morning?"

"Hunter," she said, "it's one o'clock on a Sunday afternoon." She smiled sweetly. "I'm sorry about your squirrel. What's he doing now, packing?"

I looked out again. The squirrel seemed to be trying to turn himself into a part of the tree. "I think he's trying a diversionary tactic."

"Then he's packing," she said. Jamie is a lawyer, which explains everything and nothing. As for myself, I try to do as little as possible. I write an occasional freelance story just to keep my hand in the real world, but the rest of the time I fend off every opportunity possible to travel and see exotic lands. After the insanity of two semi–best-selling

9

books and a movie deal, the only exotic land I want to see is just off my front porch.

I live on an island in the Delaware River. Jamie points out that this says damn near all there is to say about me. She may be right. Legally, I am part of New Jersey. On a good day, however, I can toss a rock and hit Pennsylvania. Years ago, after the book business blew over, I bought the island and the old run-down Victorian guesthouse on it from the bank. The bank had been trying to get rid of the property for what seemed like forever and I got it for a song.

The island is off a place called Raven Rock. Several hundred yards beyond the bridge to the mainland, there are limestone cliffs that had once served as a large rookery. The natives got tired of the birds and blew them all away one sunny afternoon in 1902. For my money, the starlings are a poor substitute.

I moved into the place with Jules, my dog, and began devoting myself to the plumbing. I was happy leading a basic Thoreau-like existence. But somewhere in my carefully laid plans Jamie appeared; I was looking for somebody as a favor for a friend and the somebody happened to be one of Jamie's clients. She has her own law firm in Princeton, something that never fails to impress me. It seems to do the same thing for her various clients.

Jamie had plans as well, and I showed up in time to toss them neatly out the window. So, there we were, just two modern folks trying to squeeze themselves into the word *relationship*.

All of a sudden, Jules shifted her considerable bulk and the table rose slightly as if in the middle of a séance. I grabbed my coffee cup before it fell over. The second section of the *Times* fell on the floor, and Jules attacked it immediately. Then the phone rang.

"The phone," Jamie said, trying to take the paper away from the dog.

"Good guess," I said.

"Are you going to get it?"

"I'm going to consider it," I said, knowing I wasn't going

to do anything of the sort. If it was the President and he wanted my advice, he would call back.

Jamie gave up on the paper and got the phone. Jules munched happily on the Arts and Leisure section.

"Yo, dog!" I said and pointed to the paper. Jules ignored me.

"It's for you," Jamie said and sat down at the table, after calmly taking the paper away from Jules. I know when I'm outnumbered and went into the kitchen to talk to the President.

"Hello, Hunter?" a voice said when I picked it up. "You son of a bitch, how are you?"

"I'm just peachy. Who's this?"

"This is Rodger."

"Rodger who?"

"Rodger from Detroit."

"Oh," I said, "Rodger from Detroit. I thought you'd be in jail for molesting spandex or something. Where are you?"

"In New York."

My God, I thought, the boy's within shooting distance. His full name was Rodger Klein and he was the editor of the magazine at the *Detroit Free Press* in the late '60s when I was there. Rodger looked like Clark Kent but his brain was a toss-up between Pinky Lee and Lenny Bruce. We all thought he was a rubber freak at home.

Rodger was heavily into creative supervision, and he put me to work on the geek beat for the magazine. I wrote one of my favorite stories for him, a compendium of what we called Destruction Art, a genre that reached its zenith in a field outside of Walled Lake. A group of local zanies bought an entire house in Livonia, a Detroit suburb that looks as if it were built for Mattel. They filled the house with bad furniture and fuzzy chartreuse rugs shaped like big feet, moved it out of the neighborhood on a tractor trailer, replanted it in the middle of the field and detonated the sucker. It was a display of glorious foolishness, and I loved every minute of it. So did Rodger. I hadn't spoken to him in years.

"Rodger from New York now. What in heaven's name are you doing?"

"Editing, what else?"

"A prison weekly?"

"Where is this prison shit coming from?"

"It's a joke, Rodger."

"I don't get it," he said, "so I know it's not important. I joined the *Times*, the magazine. I might have some work for you."

"I'm listening."

"Does that mean you're interested?"

"I'm still listening."

"Okay," he said. "An old art history prof of mine called the other day and said he wanted to talk to me. Dr. Breton—Princeton. Ring any bells?"

"Not a note. But gee, Rodger, it sounds terribly interesting so far. Tell me more."

"I couldn't get away. So I asked him to give me a few more details and I'd send somebody over if it sounded good. I thought about you—you live near there, don't you?"

"Spiritually, I live on the other side of the universe."

"Don't go rural on me, Hunter. I think there's a story in it."

"In what, Rodger?"

"Russian ikons. Religious paintings. Christ on a cross, spiritual stuff, you know."

"I don't know anything about ikons or Russians—except that they're crazy."

"Washington is crazy, too," he said vaguely.

"This is not news. What about ikons?"

"Someone's been stealing some of them. He refused to tell me anything more than that."

That was about all Rodger told me. Except that he couldn't pay me unless I found a story in it but if there was a story he'd pay expenses and a nice sum. It was January; winter had settled in; Jules likes to eat; I could use a few bucks. I agreed.

"All right," I said, "I'll look him up. So, what have you been doing with yourself, Rodger?"

"Nothing much."

"I find that difficult to believe."

"I joined a commune in Texas for a while," he said.

12

"Good God, Rodger, what kind of communes do they have in Texas?"

"We worshiped armadillos and ate a lot of peyote. Mostly we did peyote."

"That sounds sick, even for you."

"Oh, it was," he said gleefuly. "I did that for a while and kind of traveled around for a while."

"And emerged at the *Times*."

"Talent, Hunter, raw talent. Even a few months of chewing peyote can't change that."

"It must have given the *Times* an uncertain moment or two."

"I told them I was researching a novel," he said. "They loved it."

"Smart move," I said, "You think there's a story on the ikons?"

"Breton is a real ikon freak. He wrote a couple of books about them—classics. And he sounded very agitated on the phone. That intrigued me. He's usually so far out of things he just floats along."

"Why would anyone steal a Russian ikon?"

"That's what I'm paying you to find out, Hunter."

"Rodger," I said, "you're not paying me, remember?"

"Metaphorically," he said.

Metaphorically, my butt. I wanted to ask him the last time he tried to buy anything with a metaphor, but then, Rodger had been into peyote.

"When do I see him?"

"I made an appointment for you tonight." I took down the details and Rodger said good-bye. I felt absurdly pleased with myself. It was nice to be employed again even if the possibility of being paid for it was only hinted at somewhere far down the line.

I went back into the greenhouse and told Jamie.

"Ikons," she said. "What do you know about ikons?"

"I know some are missing."

"Missing from where, Hunter?"

"Jamie, it's a little vague at this point."

"The professor knows who stole them?"

"He knows something."

"What did Rodger say?"

"He said I was to go to his house and talk to him about it."

Jamie frowned. "When?"

"Tonight."

"I thought we were going out tonight," she said.

"Shit," I said.

"It's a very common word." She went into the kitchen for more coffee. "What time is your meeting with the professor?"

"Around seven."

"Okay," she said, "when will you be finished?"

"I don't know."

"Shit," Jamie said.

Outside, the squirrel had come down from his perch and was getting chased around the yard by the starlings again. He stood up on his little hind legs and chattered furiously at them. The fool. They sideswiped his head again and he retreated to another tree. He was developing a nervous twitch from all the attention. Couldn't blame him.

Jamie had her head buried in the paper.

"Haven't you read that section already?" I said stupidly.

Jamie lowered the paper.

"Hunter," she said, "do you read lips?"

"No."

"Try this," she said and blew me a perfect raspberry.

2

IT WAS bitter cold as I walked up the street to Breton's house, the snow squeaking under my boots. The professor lived in a neighborhood just off the campus. From where I stood, I could see the high stone buildings of Princeton rising up over the tops of the houses and the bare winter trees. Most of the buildings on the Princeton campus resemble cathedrals, and the effect of all that stone is constipating. No wonder some kid tried to make a nuclear bomb there.

Breton lived in a large two-story frame house with several evergreens arranged haphazardly in front of the wide open porch. He didn't shovel his walk. The snow was crusted and stamped down in a narrow path to the steps. I navigated to the front door and rang the bell, and I waited. Nobody came. I waited some more. I began to get frostbite in my fingers, so I went around to the side and banged on the back door.

After a while, the door opened the length of the chain. "What do you want?" said a woman with a heavy Russian accent.

There was a halo of light behind her head, and all I could see were her eyes, large, round saucers, blinking rapidly.

"I rang the bell but nobody answered," I said, snapping on my happy face. "I came to see Professor Breton. He's expecting me."

"Give me your name," she said.

"Hunter," I told her, and she shut the door in my happy face. A few minutes later, she opened it and let me inside, apologizing profusely.

"I am sorry," she said. "I did not know he had an appointment tonight. He never tells me these things. I am expected to read his mind. You are the writer. My name is Vera. I am his housekeeper."

Vera was a short round woman who carried her blank expression around like a shield. She walked in quick half-steps, leading me through the kitchen and into a pleasant, jumbled study in the back of the house, smoothing out her plain brown dress as she went. Her only concession to fashion was a small curl that seemed to hover over one eye.

"He is working in the basement," Vera said. "He will be with you soon. Would you like something from the kitchen? Coffee? Some tea?"

"Tea, I think."

"With lemon?"

"No, milk."

"You are English?"

"I'm kind of a mongrel."

Vera accepted my heritage silently and went into the kitchen. I prowled through Breton's study.

On the wall over his desk was an ikon. It was the figure of Christ, drawn from the waist up. His right hand was raised in a three-finger benediction. In the other hand, he held a book. The writing on the book was Russian. The background of the painting was bright gold. His robe was nearly the same color, the lines etched in beautifully.

The face was a surprise. It was a kindly, half-smiling face, like that of a favorite uncle I'd had. In the darkness of the study, the small ikon gave the room a monastical glow.

The rest of the room was lined with books, some in English, some in Russian. There was a heavy reclining chair at one end with a small coffee table next to it. Books and papers lay in a pile on top of the table, but the desk was clean. Never trust a man with a clean desk, I thought.

Professor Breton said, "It's from the seventeenth century. The Moscow School. 'Christ Pantokrator.' "

Breton was wearing an apron covered with stains and pockmarked with holes, as though he'd applied battery acid all over it. He was a man of medium size with a square head and black glasses. In one hand he was holding a pair of rubber gloves. He seemed upset that I was there.

"It's lovely," I said.

"Lovely?" he said as if the word were new to him. "It's a

16

funeral ikon. Usually they were made up by young painters, apprentices. This is an exception. An exquisite piece. I'm working on another one right now."

"Is this a bad time?"

"No, no," he said, waving the rubber gloves at me. "I simply forgot you were coming."

Breton looked at his watch.

"Excuse me," he said and walked out of the study. I took this to mean I could tag along at my own risk. I followed him through the kitchen and down a short flight of stairs to the basement. He hardly even noticed I was there. His workshop was small and had a harsh, corrosive odor that made my eyes water. Clamped to the workbench in the middle of the room was another ikon.

A large weight was sitting on top of a square piece of glass on one corner of the ikon. Carefully, Breton lifted up the weight and then the glass. Some fabric came away with the glass. He stared at the spot, then picked up a small paring knife and began cleaning it off. Bright gold appeared. The rest of the ikon was nearly black, with the vague outlines of a figure beneath the blackness. The surface shimmered.

Breton kept staring at the spot and shook his head. He cut a piece of heavy flannel cloth from a larger sheet, dunked it in some foul-smelling liquid and placed it over the spot. Then he put the glass down on it and laid the weight on the glass.

"Do you have any idea what I'm doing?" he asked.

"My first guess would be you're cleaning it up."

Breton smiled patiently. People just have no tolerance for the obvious these days.

"I had hoped this was a little older," he said, "but I don't think so. It's nineteenth-century junk. But there may be more underneath."

"Of course," I said. "Underneath."

Breton stared at me over his glasses. "I'll try to explain it to you. When ikons were first painted, they were covered with a thin coat of oil to protect the image. What the oil really did was create a sticky surface that picked up dirt, ash, anything that fell on it. After a few decades, the surface turned black. Do you know what they call ikons in Russia?"

"Fred and Ethel?"

"Who are Fred and Ethel?" he asked.

I shook my head and asked him to continue.

"They're called black boards, Mr. Hunter," he said. "When the image became too black, they simply painted a new one over it. This practice went on for centuries." He tapped the surface of the ikon. "What you have are layers of paint, each with a separate image, all from different times. See this little lip around the edge?"

Breton ran his finger down a narrow ridge that ran around the ikon.

"That makes me think it's old. But it could merely be a good imitation. After the seventeenth century, ikon painting was left to people who had no inspiration, no vision. They tried to make up for it by relying on technique."

He removed the weight and the glass. Another image appeared, similar, but a richer, deeper shade of gold.

"Definitely eighteenth-century," he said. "Perhaps I was wrong."

I controlled myself, and did not yell "Far out!"

He went through the ritual with the flannel, the glass and the weight again. This time we didn't talk. He stared at the ikon as though it were about to give up something miraculous. Maybe he thought it was going to sing and dance.

Finally, what appeared beneath the flannel was pure white, no image, no gold, no nothing. He took off a rubber glove and pinched his eyes.

"Junk," he said. He threw the apron on the floor. "Nothing but junk."

"What is it?"

"That," he said, "is gesso. Alabaster and glue. The original base. It means this is eighteenth-century and nothing more. As I said, junk."

Breton looked like a man who'd been told his firstborn had just become a Moonie. I followed him out of the basement and back into the study.

"I would not have called Rodger," Breton said, "if I didn't have a suspicion that something was going on. I am

18

really not the hysterical old man that he thinks I am, you know."

"He didn't say that, professor. Not to me, at least."

"Oh," he said, feigning disinterest. "What did he say?"

"He said you thought there was an ikon missing somewhere and that I should look into it. He took your suspicion seriously, that's all. He said you were an expert."

"Hmmmpf," Breton said, pleased. He sat on the edge of the chair and fiddled with the sleeve of his sweater, mentally preening his reputation. I sipped my tea and waited for lightning to strike me dead.

"Ikons," Breton said, "several, in fact. Over the last three years, up and down the East Coast. Someone has been stealing ikons."

"Where were they taken from?"

"Churches. Where else?"

"Homes, private collections, galleries? I didn't think people kept them in package stores."

"Do you know what an ikon is?" He gave me his stern gaze, the one he must have used on hopelessly dumb students.

"They look like religious paintings to me."

"Wrong!" he thundered. He was working up to a full-scale lecture, and I was certain he expected me to take notes. I took out my notebook and wrote down the word "wrong." Jamie feels this is my whole approach to living.

"An ikon is a religious painting, true," he said, "but it's much more than that. In its purest sense, it's like a window to God. People don't pray to ikons, they pray to God *through* the painted image. Did you know that in the eighth and ninth centuries, ikons were destroyed because they were thought to be a form of idolatry? Can you imagine? Thousands of ikons were burned and smashed because some fool thought they were sinful."

I tried to act sympathetic. Breton obviously took it as a personal tragedy.

"Where was this exactly?" I said cheerfully.

Heavy sigh of frustration from Professor Breton.

"Byzantium," he said. "It was the Byzantines who carried ikonography to Russia. But in Russia—after it be-

19

came Christian under Vladimir—they developed their own style. They achieved great art."

At the word "art," I perked right up.

"Then they must be valuable," I said. "That would explain the thefts."

"Not necessarily," Breton said. "Some are valuable, some aren't. The ones that were stolen over the last three years were not. There are few, if any, really valuable ikons around. The highest price ever paid for one was around one hundred and seventy thousand dollars—for a sixteenth-century ikon, very rare. Of course, the Russians have kept the best for themselves. After spending years trying to wipe them out by burning churches and killing priests, someone realized that ikons were a national treasure." He gazed at the ikon over his desk. "But the damage was done. The Russians are a thoughtless race.

"But if someone were to come across an old ikon, from the thirteenth century or even fourteenth—my God, even the fifteenth—it would be a priceless discovery."

"But you said there weren't/any more around."

Breton smiled curiously. "I thought so as well. Until someone took the ikon I discovered in Hermitage."

"I've heard that name before," I said.

"It's here, in New Jersey. A sort of homing place for a lot of old White Russians, the ones who came here after the Civil War. One of their generals is buried up there."

"I don't remember hearing that much about it."

"I'm not surprised. Most people haven't. They keep to themselves, the Russians. They don't mix, not even with the other people in town. Most of Hermitage is on the Jersey side, but there are bits scattered across the border in New York. A very odd place."

"How did you find the ikon there?"

"By accident," he said. "It was in the church—St. Sergius'. I spent some time there last year, talking with several of the people but mostly with the priest, Father Nicholas. Interesting man, who works very hard at keeping the place going. Terribly difficult. Most of the Russians in his congregation are old, and the young ones are moving away. Of course, Kharkovnakov's there."

20

"The writer? I know he was exiled by the Soviets in the early '60s, one of the first."

"He's not that well known any longer," Breton said. "Not like Solzhenitsyn, although I think he's the better writer. He has his own view of things, very similar but more radical. The original Slavophile, despises the communists and the West."

"I remember he made one or two speeches here. People thought he was crazy."

"Journalists," Breton said, blowing the word out through his nose. "He's still quite a powerful voice, despite what the newspapers say, especially in the church."

"What about the ikon?"

"Oh, yes, the ikon. Let me show you a picture."

He went to the bookshelf and pulled down a thick volume, mumbling to himself as he flipped the pages. "Here," he said. It was an ikon of Christ, but only his face. The head was circled by a halo against a background of translucent yellow, the skin a light delicate brown. It was the only thing delicate about the picture. Christ's expression was hard, unforgiving.

"It's an early ikon form," Breton said. "Called 'The Savior Painted Without Hands.' It's quite different from the one hanging over there."

"Is this the one that was stolen?"

"No, this one hangs in the Tretyakov Gallery in Moscow. Thirteenth-century—from Novgorod. An exceptionally fine study, don't you think?"

"*I* wouldn't steal it."

Breton closed the book.

"Then you'd be a fool," he said. "An ikon like this would be worth somewhere in the vicinity of half a million dollars."

"Is the missing ikon worth that much?"

"I don't really know. The ikon in St. Sergius' was very similar to this. I say similar because I was forbidden to examine it. I couldn't even photograph it. But I think that it was old—quite old. There was something else. It's pure speculation, of course."

Breton's voice had taken on an aura of mystery, a soft downturn in tone.

"What I'm alluding to is a legend, hundreds of years old, about a series of ikons like the one I saw in the church. They were supposedly painted by an outcast monk named Fyodor sometime in the thirteenth century." He smiled mischievously, clearly enjoying himself. "The legend claims that Fyodor used his own blood to paint the ikons."

"Do you believe the legend?"

"I don't necessarily disbelieve it."

"But is it possible?"

"Anything is possible in Russia," he said. "You see, the early monks were often strange and fanatical men. They hid out in the woods, lived in caves, practicing self-flagellation and all that. Using one's own blood might not be that unusual. Some even claim that Fyodor's ikons bled."

"Stigmata," I said, and saw Breton raise an eyebrow. I had moved up a notch in his estimation. I knew an obscure word.

"Yes," he said. "Again, not an unusual claim. The problem is, none of Fyodor's ikons were ever found. Some scholars maintain they never existed at all. Others say they were destroyed after the revolution. One or two claim to have seen records of them in the Kremlin. It's a legend, and legends are always very difficult to verify."

"Are you trying to verify this one?"

"Someone certainly is. They thought enough of it to take the ikon from St. Sergius."

"Did you say anything to the priest about the legend?"

"I mentioned it in passing, just to test the waters. He dismissed it completely."

"Who might have taken it?"

"I really don't know."

"One of your colleagues? Another scholar?"

"Scholars do not make a habit of stealing, Mr. Hunter," he said sharply.

"Then who?"

"There are others who might have an interest in it. One or two collectors I can think of, possibly the Soviets themselves, though I doubt it sincerely. They have more ikons than they need. In any case, I'm not going to go any further—at least for the moment. I don't approve of gossip and I don't involve myself in slander. Father Nicholas may

22

help you, he may not. If he doesn't, come back and we'll discuss it."

"Did he tell you the ikon was stolen?"

Breton shifted uncomfortably in his chair.

"No," he said. "I received a phone call two weeks ago. From whom I don't know. It was simply a Russian voice telling me that the ikon was missing. Of course, I called Father Nicholas. He confirmed that it was missing but said they were hoping to get it back. He implied that it was some sort of internecine squabble. That happens more often in the Orthodox church than you might suspect. The American church doesn't care for the church in Moscow, and there are various sects and splinter groups all vying for control. It's quite fascinating."

"This isn't a lot to go on, professor."

"Don't you think you should talk to Father Nicholas first? If it *is* one of the Fyodor ikons, it would be a stunning discovery. You really have no idea."

I was almost certain of that.

As I left Breton's house, I saw a figure crouched near the front porch. As I walked down the driveway, the figure moved from the corner and scurried across the yard.

I kept walking down the sidewalk, past my jeep to the end of the street. When I turned around, no one was there. The street was perfectly still. I went back to the jeep and opened the door.

Vera stepped out from behind the hood and whispered loudly, "I must talk to you." I backed up against the open door and began to swear. If I'd had a handful of garlic I would have waved it at her.

Vera crossed herself immediately. "Please," she whispered. "I'm sorry if I frightened you. I could not talk inside. Please, help me."

"Get in the car," I said and started up the engine. We shivered in silence until the jeep warmed up. Vera cowered in the seat, her eyes downcast.

"He told you about the ikon," she said.

"He told me one was missing from the church in Hermitage."

Vera shook her head. "Stolen," she said.

"What do you know about it, Vera?"

She looked at me suspiciously and said, "Turn on the radio, please. Make noise."

I turned it on but kept the volume down.

"Please, louder, more noise." She said it desperately, glancing over the dash at the street. I turned it up a little higher.

When it reached the proper volume, she turned, fingers twisting out toward my arm. "They will kill him for what he knows about the ikon."

"Who's going to kill him?"

"I cannot tell you," she said and looked out the window again.

"Then how do you know?"

"Please," she said, "I know. You must find it and return it."

"Vera," I said, "I can't do anything if you won't tell me *anything.*"

She spoke rapidly.

"There was a call while he was out. They told me to say that if he did not forget what he had heard about the ikon, they would kill him."

"Did you tell him about the call?"

"No," she said. "I was frightened."

"Was it a Russian?"

She lowered her head. "Yes." Then, looking up at me, she said, "You do not believe me. You think I am just a foolish old woman. But I know what I hear, I know."

"I don't think you made it up, Vera. But maybe it was a joke. Maybe the whole thing's a joke."

She buried her head in her hands and said something I couldn't understand. Suddenly, she opened the door and jumped out.

"Wait," I said, and I grabbed for her, but it was too late. She began running back to the house. I threw open my door and ran after her. She stopped a few yards from the jeep and crossed herself rapidly. She spun around to face me.

Her skin seemed to absorb the light, turning it white and hard as bone. She was more frightened than anyone I had seen in years.

She clutched the collar of her coat and whispered, "The Old Believers. The Old Believers will kill him."

I tried to reach her, but she darted away.

"They will kill us all," she said and ran back to the house, to the safety of the darkness.

3

THERE WAS A note on the kitchen table from Jamie that said, "Dear Rude Person. I waited around hoping that you might be home a little early. No such luck. I went to visit Lucy and will be back sometime before sunrise."

Jules had crawled onto the couch and gave me her standard baleful eye. She's a large dog, about the size of a sedan, and when she decides to sleep on the couch, nothing short of an earthquake will budge her. She made no effort to be friends, even when I brought out the box of Dog Whoopees and shook it in her direction. Jules has all the loyalty of a hundred-dollar bill.

I took some chicken from the freezer and hammered it on the counter top until it broke into several little blocks of ice. I shook it up with some seasoned flour, most of which refused to stick, and dropped it in a frying pan of hot oil. It was going to be a wonderful meal. With any luck, it would be interrupted by half a dozen crazed monks who would cart me off to a cave to do disgusting things to my body, not to mention my chicken.

While I endured third-degree burns from the spitting oil, I tried to put the situation in perspective. I had a stolen ikon—maybe—that might have been painted by a geek named Fyodor—maybe—that might be worth an enormous amount of money—maybe—and a group called the Old Believers who might be ready to butcher everybody in their sleep if I didn't find the allegedly stolen ikon which might not have been stolen in the first place and return it to them, whoever *they* were.

That was an awful lot of questions for an assignment that to date had paid me exactly zilch. With that thought, I went into my biannual cursing of editors. Editors hate to pay you because they have this curiously twisted notion that writers would write even if they were starving to death, which they usually are. I knew of several editors I would like to see encased in Lucite—like quarters in a toilet seat. I should be going back to school to learn how to program computers.

I read Jamie's note again and wished she were there with me. Every time we have a fight, I immediately think: I don't need this in my life. That lasts for approximately five minutes. Afterward, I miss her like crazy. I hope she never catches on to it.

I laid the fried chicken to rest on my plate and listened to an old Neil Young tape, a nice high lonesome one that he made before he fell under the influence of amphetamine rock and started churning out stuff that could rupture spleens from half a mile away. Jules felt in a forgiving mood and waddled over. I fed her a couple pieces of chicken, and she laid her big head on my knee.

Outside, the wind picked up and the windows groaned. The ice on the river kept shifting, stretching and cracking like a loose wooden hull and the sound sliced through the room. Jules whipped her head around at the noise and roamed nervously through the house. I thought I heard voices somewhere in the night.

Old Believers. I saw them dressed in black cassocks carrying candles and shiny axes, eyes like fire trapped in glass jars. Like a fool, I locked the front door.

I am all alone out here, I thought. I could end up quick-frozen, sitting in my living room like a Sara Lee coffee cake until spring and nobody would know.

I have too vivid an imagination. It was ten-thirty and Jamie wasn't home. I had eaten two small pieces of chicken and didn't want any more. Jules had returned to the couch, so I grabbed a cushion and settled down on the rug. I was asleep in about five minutes, dreaming bad dreams.

I was in a large dark building. Men in cassocks were chasing me, their eyes leaping out of black skulls. I couldn't get away. Something grabbed at my arm.

Jamie was sitting on the floor next to me, saying my name. I sat up and shook my head.

"Are you all right?" she asked.

"I was dreaming."

"You were shaking all over," she said. "It must have been a nightmare."

"I was being chased by a bunch of crazy people."

"That's not unusual for you, Hunter," she said. "I'm sorry about the note."

"I'm the one who forgot about dinner. How's Lucy?"

"She's fine. Busy scraping walls and making Red Devil Chili."

Lucy's Red Devil Chili was legend along the river. After two days, it could be used to strip furniture.

"I thought of something driving back," Jamie said. "Do you know I haven't been home in four days, and half the clothes I own are in the bottom drawer of your dresser?"

"And?"

"And nothing, I just thought of it, that's all."

I know enough not to press her on anything. Twenty years ago, we would have been married and she would have been pregnant. And I'd have been fighting my slow and deliberate way up some thorny corporate ladder. Instead, we circle around each other, analyzing each step we take, with one eye on the clock and another on the door. A modern "relationship."

"Want to hear about my meeting with the professor?" I asked Jamie.

"Tomorrow," she said. "Right now I want to go to bed with you."

She kissed me and pulled me slowly off the floor. Jules followed us up the stairs like an only child. At the top, she turned and said, "Hunter, have I told you today that I loved you?"

Come to think of it, she hadn't.

The next day Jamie insisted upon exercising her rights by going with me to Hermitage. "I gave up a night on the town and I'm going with you," she said. Even if it meant driving fifty-odd miles and missing a day of work. Besides, she said, she knew a little bit of Russian history from her undergraduate days. We stopped by her house and picked up some old textbooks. Lawyers don't say anything unless they can find it written down somewhere else.

We drove up Route 31 toward the Delaware Water Gap.

New Jersey in its infinite wisdom has seen fit to put in a lot of LeMans-type hairpin curves and blind passing zones which add just the right amount of institutionalized terror to your morning drive.

We got off 31 and headed up a narrow two-lane road that ran through a valley next to a line of mountains. For a while, resort signs dominated the landscape, then they thinned out. The snow was piled high on the sides of the road, and the trees were sharp and crisp against a clear blue sky. I was mesmerized, content to watch the world unfold.

We passed a sign that said: *Caution! Evergreens coated with noxious spray!* So much for the forest primeval.

Jamie skimmed her books. "I know there's something about Hermitage," she said. "I just wish I could remember it."

"I want to know about the Old Believers," I said.

"I'm getting to that. Here we are. Old Believers. They didn't appear in Russia until the last part of the seventeenth century under Archibishop Nikon."

"The man who invented the camera," I said.

She ignored me. "Nikon changed the church liturgy. That was his big mistake. A lot of priests called his reforms heresy and refused to endorse them. Nikon didn't much care for their objections."

"What was his response?"

"The usual. He had a few thousand burned at the stake. The rest he just hauled off to prison."

"Sensible precautions."

"That was how the Old Believers got started. They kept the old litugry and worshiped in secret. A few of them actually killed themselves—they burned themselves to death in the churches."

"Nothing like the art of meaningful compromise to get you through the centuries. Obviously they survived."

"Apparently they reached some kind of agreement with Moscow. They got through the revolution—barely—and they're still around. Even in Russia. There's a small group of them in Hermitage and another out in Oregon."

"Tenacity is important if you're going to make it in the lunatic fringe."

We drove for a while. Jamie paged through the book.

"Did you know that Kharkovnakov lives in Hermitage?"

"My God," she said. "I thought he was dead. Is he still alive?"

"That's what Breton told me."

"Do you think we can go see him?" she said excitedly.

"We can try."

"Oh," she said, "I'd love to meet him. I adore his books. They're all about the Russian soul."

"Name me a Russian writer who hasn't written about the Russian soul."

"Leonid Brezhnev," she said. "Kharkovnakov wrote a trilogy—*The Birches, The Steppes* and *The River*. He said that's what made up the Russian character."

She found a passage in her textbook and read it to me.

" 'The woods weighed heavily on the soul of the Russian people. It seemed to convey a secret threat—the eerie atmosphere put the woodsman's nerves on edge.' I think that's pretty neat."

"I do, too," I said.

"The steppes meant freedom," she said, "infinite freedom—and danger. Russia was invaded from the steppes—the Mongol hordes and their ilk. The river is the most peaceful symbol—the Russian community, their home." She closed her book and sighed. "Oh, Hunter, I loved those books. We just have to try to see him."

"Maybe he doesn't want to see anybody," I said. "He was exiled, remember."

"I know that. He flowered under Khrushchev, and when he went out, so did Kharkovnakov. Especially when they realized what he was doing."

"All he did was write books, I thought."

"He did more than that. He wanted to clean out the bureaucrats and start over. Except he wanted the people to go back to their farms and forget about technology and communism and all the other isms. He wanted a religious dictatorship."

"In other words, he wanted to turn Russia into one big Iran."

"Absolutely," she said. "I still think he should've won

the Nobel. He was never imprisoned, not like Solzhenitsyn. They just shut him up in a little house somewhere and refused to acknowledge his existence. They banned his books and gave him a job as a Russian forest ranger or something. He got kicked out before it became the fashionable thing to do. Nobody's heard from him in ten years."

She closed her book and stared out the window.

"I was madly in love with him when I was nineteen," she said. "I wanted to run away and live with him."

"You are a sap—sometimes."

She smiled. "Yes, I am—sometimes. His books were so romantic. You never read them?"

"No."

"They were a saga about two Russian families. One sticks to the old ways and the other embraces the revolution. They fight, intermarry, die, get born—saga things. The last book, at least the ending, was a little depressing."

"What happened in the last book?"

"The young son of the revolutionary family—he was studying to be a doctor and gave it all up for Marx and Lenin—marries the young daughter of the Old Believer family. When he finds out she's been spying on him, telling her brother or whoever she tells, about what the Bolsheviks are going to do to the church, he kills her. Strangles her in her own bed. It drives him mad and he wanders off into the Russian night, babbling to himself."

"Sounds pleasant."

"It was the last scene in the book and it seemed to sum up the choices Kharkovnakov thought the Russian people had to make. Between death and insanity. It was utterly gruesome. He described the death scene in excruciating detail. I still cringe when I think about it."

We crossed over a small creek and headed up a hill. On the other side, a golden dome topped with a cross suddenly floated into view over the tops of the trees, followed by two small domes of a darker color. I slowed down. The dome seemed to explode in the bright sunlight. I pulled the car to the side of the road and stopped. In seconds, we had been hurtled back through time, to another era, another place.

"Wow," I said.

Jamie looked at me in astonishment.

31

"I don't believe you just said that." She held up her hands as if cradling an undersized trout. "Wow," she mimicked and tried to keep from smirking.

It was going to be one of those days. I could just tell.

We drove slowly past the church. The white stucco walls rose up in curved arches toward the three domes and the crosses. The other two domes were painted a deep enamel blue; small golden stars floated through them. Each cross had two bars at the top and a third bar across the middle, angled toward the earth. At the bottom of each cross was a half-circle, making them seem like anchors. Surrounding the church on three sides was a cemetery, row upon row of gray and pinkish stones that seemed to stretch out for miles.

A small group of people in dark coats and fur hats were walking out of the cemetery, their heads bowed down, white clouds of breath vanishing into the cold air. They looked up and stared as we drove by. In the distance, I could see Hermitage.

Jamie said, "Look over there."

I followed the line of her finger to the left. On the side of the mountain, high up, stood a house. I could barely see it through the wall of white birches that surrounded it like some ancient fortress.

"Kharkovnakov," I whispered. Jamie stared at the house. Fifteen minutes later, I parked the car in Hermitage.

Hermitage was a single street that followed the line of the mountains through the valley. On the mountain side, the rear of the stores opened onto an incline of great trees and boulders that jutted up through the snow. On the other side, the town spread out into the valley, quiet streets filled with homes. The smell of woodsmoke drifted through the air.

It was a clean, well-ordered town. The sidewalks were clear, piles of snow placed carefully at the end of each block. The people drove slowly and parked their cars at neat angles against the curb. They nodded at us and went about their business. We picked out a small coffee shop across from where we parked and were walking toward it when Jamie stopped in the middle of the street.

"I just remembered," she said excitedly.

"Let's remember on the sidewalk," I said.

"No, no," she said, "I remembered about Hermitage. It was five or six years ago." She grabbed my elbow. "They caught a spy here."

"And I want to hear about it," I said. "Inside, where I don't have to freeze to death to be fascinated."

It turned out the spy's name was Dimitri and he had been a Russian sailor who jumped ship in Elizabeth, New Jersey. He wasn't terribly bright, but the newspapers fell all over him and his leap for freedom, a leap which resulted in two broken legs because the dodo didn't have the sense to aim for the water.

Dimitri hit the New Jersey bulkhead from about twenty-five feet up and crawled on his hands and knees to a group of longshoremen who didn't move until he got close enough to make his dramatic rescue convenient. Later they said they didn't want to get in trouble with the union. Dimitri would have had better luck if he'd been in a container.

In any event, they put Dimitri in the hospital, gave him a checking account, two tons worth of appliances, new clothes, and a new car. The local car dealer made a big deal out of it, posing alongside Dimitri in his half-body cast, graciously clutching the keys to a new Montego in his big meaty hand.

A week or so after he got out of the cast, Dimitri rediscovered vodka, got drunk and drove the Montego into a phone booth, a fire hydrant and a nearby porch. Dimitri managed to escape without a scratch. He did not, however, receive a second Montego. And since he didn't have a driver's license, they couldn't suspend it. The judge told him to lay off the vodka and let him walk.

Dimitri walked directly to Hermitage and the Russian community, where he spent several months getting drunk and throwing up on his fellow exiles, filling in the spaces by doing odd jobs such as fixing washing machines and running errands for the remnants of the aristocracy. He got a driver's license and a used Buick and began lecturing to high-school audiences about the evils of communism. He spoke a half-witted, impenetrable English and put teenagers to sleep all across the state.

He also came in contact with a lot of people who worked in the high-tech companies in northern New Jersey. At that point, Dimitri asked one of the engineers if he wanted to make some extra money by exchanging top-secret plans for big bucks. The engineer went straight to the FBI and they went straight to Dimitri and locked the poor bastard away after making another big deal about catching a red-hot Russian agent.

Dimitri vanished less spectacularly than he arrived, and that was the last anybody ever heard about him. Jamie told all this to me over the dollar-fifty breakfast special, minus the juice. She was a little disappointed when I didn't yell "Stop the presses!" or whatever.

"I thought it was interesting," she said.

"It is, but somehow I don't think the Russians spend a great deal of their time sending idiots like Dimitri around to steal ikons. I think he got in over his head and drowned."

The waitress came by with more coffee.

"The big house on the mountain—the one with all the birches?" Jamie asked her.

"That's Zemlya. The writer lives up there."

"Kharkovnakov," I said.

"That's him. Doesn't come down at all. Funny name, isn't it? For a house, I mean."

"It means 'land' in Russian," Jamie said.

"Really," the waitress said. "Isn't that interesting."

After she left, Jamie said, "She sounds about as impressed with my knowledge as you do."

"I didn't know you were a closet Russophile."

"Pay the check, Hunter," she said.

Outside, she said, "Zemlya means more than just 'land'. The Russian Zemlya—the holy earth, the motherland. It fits him."

"You are a constant amazement to me," I said.

I could hear her counting to ten mentally.

"Hunter," she said, "you have the spiritual content of a beer can."

34

We drove back to the church to find Father Nicholas.

The church doors were locked and a sign on the door said:

HEED! WHOSOEVER ENTERS THE HOUSE OF GOD. A WOMAN SHALL NOT BE CLOTHED WITH MAN'S APPAREL, NEITHER SHALL A MAN USE WOMEN'S APPAREL: FOR HE THAT DOETH THESE THINGS IS ABOMINABLE BEFORE GOD.

DEUTERONOMY, 22, 5.

I looked at Jamie's jeans.

"You're not going to be invited in for tea," I said.

"Wait'll I tell them about your flimsy peignoir at home."

"You wouldn't."

"And the silk chemise, too."

"You're cruel."

"But interesting," she said. "What do we do now, Ace?"

"See the sights," I said.

We walked through the cemetery, down the neat, orderly rows. We stopped at one grave that had three miniature gold domes on top. It turned out to be that of a priest who was laid to rest next to his wife. Some of the stones had small black-and-white photographs of their occupants. A few had pictures of Christ. The names were in Russian and English—Sheshko, Avraloff, Kozloff.

There was one grave set off from the others with a bust on top of the stone. In profile, he looked a little like the czar, right down to the goatee.

"That's Marokov," Jamie said, "A White Russian general. He led the civil war."

"And lost," I pointed out.

"Not entirely. He managed to escape with a small fortune in gold and gems, something he plucked out of the treasury for a rainy day."

It was quiet in the cemetery, perhaps a little sad. A bright-red cardinal, poor fool out of place, flitted across the stones on his way to the woods behind us. I heard a noise, a door slammed shut, and saw a heavyset man in a gray workman's coat start across the cemetery toward us. Jamie didn't hear it, lost in the serenity of the place. I hoped

35

he was friendly. He looked as if someone had forgotten to give him his daily feeding.

His black wool hat was pulled down over a wide flat face. Each step seemed slow and deliberate. He stopped a few feet from us with his hands in his pockets, blocking the way. We could either go around him or through him, and he didn't seem inclined to allow either. His voice was a low rumble.

"What do you want?"

"We came to see Father Nicholas."

"Not here."

"I know. We tried the church."

"Come back later. Tonight."

"Do you know where he is?"

"Gone."

"We came to talk about the ikon," I said, and he took a few steps closer.

"You have seen it?"

"No. I wanted to ask Father Nicholas some questions."

That confused him. If I hadn't seen it, why would I want to ask questions? Oh, those crazy Americans. The whole process seemed out of his jurisdiction.

"Zemlya—up there." He pointed a thumb toward the mountain.

"He's there?"

"Come back tonight," he said.

Jamie took my arm, and we walked past him. He moved to one side, and I caught a whiff of incense. I could feel his eyes on us as we headed toward the car.

"She cannot enter church," he said.

Jamie stopped. "She doesn't want to," she said and stared until he turned and walked away.

4

the post which had rattled in the trunk on a shelf. You could see it stacked snow—and if there'd been ho... with his hands in his pockets, blowing on...

ZEMLYA WAS a plateau of land high up on the mountain. Evergreens crested just above the house, held in place by the still whiteness of the birches. The road took a sharp turn in front of the plateau, and from there I could see out across the valley. The view did not decrease the sense of isolation, but seemed to exaggerate it, turning it inward to feed upon itself. No sounds were carried up from below to its gates; everything on the mountain seemed trapped by the endless blue sky.

The house itself was old, with plain wood siding, worn and pale, the color of sleet. Huddled among the birches, the original structure had been added to over the years, turning its simple lines into a sprawling jumble of squat boxes connected by narrow walkways without windows. An orange jeep was parked in front next to a black Toyota.

A woman and a big mastiff stood just inside the chain-link fence that stretched across the part of the plateau that jutted out to meet the road. The woman watched us pull up; then, as we got out, she spoke to the dog and approached the fence. The mastiff laid down in the hard-packed snow and stared out at us over the top of its nose.

She was a small woman who looked to be in her forties, brown hair, clear blue eyes and a cautious smile as though she wanted to be a good hostess but wasn't sure if it was allowed. She wore a long dark skirt over heavy boots and a brown nylon parka.

"Don't worry about Misha," she said as she opened the gate for us. "He won't bite." She snapped her fingers, and Misha lumbered over, sniffed at our clothes with indifference and stood by her side. "You came to see Father Nicholas," she said.

"The man at the cemetery—"

"He phoned and said you might be coming. Please." Jamie and I stepped inside the gate, and she closed it behind us. "My name is Kira. We don't get many visitors. My husband doesn't care for them."

She led us to the edge of the birches and pointed toward a narrow path. "Down here," she said. There were woodchips strewn over the path like pieces of confetti.

"Father Nicholas helps us out—with the cutting," she said. She spoke without an accent.

"You're not Russian," I said.

"My father was Russian, my mother was American. He came here after the war, after Stalingrad. It was either that or the camps. He was a German prisoner. Stalin thought that all prisoners were contaminated."

In the distance, I could hear the sound of a saw.

"I've read your husband's books," Jamie said.

"The trilogy? Everyone seems to have read those," Kira said.

"Does he still write?"

"He writes every day, sometimes all day. He is writing now."

"Why doesn't he publish anymore?"

"My husband doesn't wish to," she said. "My husband doesn't publish his work because he doesn't write for people anymore. My husband writes for God."

We approached a clearing. In the middle stood a tall man with close-cropped gray-blonde hair wearing a blue down vest. Another man, shorter, wearing a long black coat, stood with him. They were using a double-handled longsaw, cutting a stack of birch logs into quarters. The man in the vest waved to Kira.

"That's Father Nicholas," she said and stopped.

The first thing Father Nicholas did was laugh at me.

"Not what you expected," he said and shook my hand, then Jamie's. "Most people think I ought to have a long beard and a stern look. I haven't been successful with either."

He was cheerful and charming, completely at ease. His appearance was neither young nor old. There were tiny age lines creeping around the corners of his eyes and his mouth, but they vanished when he smiled.

We introduced ourselves, and Father Nicholas introduced the other man as Chernetzsky. He hung back by the woodpile and didn't say much. His eyes seemed to be in the process of taking our picture. Chernetzsky had a thin, angry-looking face that was barely covered by a scraggly beard. He looked like some obscure species of rat.

We stood around awkwardly until Father Nicholas said, "You mentioned the ikon."

"I'm a writer," I said and explained why I was in Hermitage. Father Nicholas nodded his head slowly.

"I wish the professor hadn't done that," he said. Chernetzsky said something to him in Russian, and he turned to the little man and spoke. Chernetzsky laughed. Kira said something to Chernetzsky, and his laughter stopped. Jamie smiled uneasily.

"I'm sorry," Father Nicholas said. "We're not trying to hide anything. It's just that the ikon has put some people on edge. We're in the process of getting it back, I hope soon. There seems to be something of a misunderstanding about its disappearance. But I'll be happy to talk to you. Tonight, after vespers."

"You still have regular vespers?" Jamie asked.

"Yes. It's an old congregation, and they still worship in the old ways. There are no Easter Christians here. I spend half my time trying to satisfy them and the other half trying to get the young people to come back to the church. I tell people I have one foot in the twentieth century and one foot in the fourteenth. It makes me a little schizophrenic at times."

"But the ikon is still missing," I said.

"Yes," he answered, "it's still missing."

"Do you have any idea where it is?"

An edge crept into his voice. "I have an idea, but I'm not going to talk about it. Anything else, yes, but the ikon, no."

I changed the subject, something I always do when someone tells me no. "You've been cutting a lot of wood."

"The people in town look up to Kharkovnakov. It helps my work if I'm associated with him. So I cut his wood. Of course, we disagree on most everything. Don't we, Kira?"

Kira smiled. "They drink vodka and argue," she said.

"My husband always wins because he can drink more vodka."

I must have looked surprised. Nicholas laughed at me again.

"You have a very old-fashioned view of priests, Mr. Hunter," he said. "After vespers, I'll see if I can enlighten you. Perhaps you'd like to come to the service. Afterward we can have dinner together."

Jamie immediately said yes. That was when Kharkovnakov emerged from the birches behind us.

He was a giant, well over six feet, dressed entirely in black, with a huge beard streaked with white that looked as if it hadn't been cut in decades. He strode over to Chernetzsky, stared down at the little man and said something in a guttural Russian that sounded very much like a direct order.

Chernetzsky nodded once and walked quickly past us down the path. Kharkovnakov watched him go. Then he turned to the priest and began yelling at him.

I saw the priest's face harden, and he yelled back.

Kharkovnakov started swinging his arms around wildly, stamping his heavy boots in the snow. Nicholas hadn't moved. He stood there and answered back, his voice growing harsh. Kharkovnakov stopped and looked directly at us. He said something to Jamie, waving a huge fist at her face.

Jamie flushed, but she waited until he finished. Finally, in a slow halting Russian, she answered him.

Kharkovnakov started toward her, and I stepped in between them. Misha took one look at me and dropped into a crouch, the muscles on the back of his neck bunched up in thick rolls.

"Misha!" Kira yelled. The dog relaxed exactly one millimeter. Kharkovnakov stopped in midstride and stared at me.

Kira grabbed Misha by the collar and yanked the dog up hard. Everyone stood frozen in place. Kira smacked the dog hard on the snout, and Misha snapped his head away. Kharkovnakov said something to Nicholas, spit on the ground at my feet, and stomped back into the birches.

40

Jamie said, "I'll wait for you in the car." Kira pulled Misha away by his collar and hurried after her.

Nicholas sighed. "Welcome to the fourteenth century," he said.

"I didn't think it was going to be so much fun," I said.

Jamie was sitting in the car, staring angrily out the window at me.

"What was that all about?" I said, getting inside.

"Nothing," she said. "Please, Hunter, let's get out of here.

"I want to know what he said to you."

"He called me several names. I didn't catch all of them. My Russian is a little rusty, but I heard enough. I told him he was a pig. Okay? Now can we just leave?"

"I didn't know you spoke Russian."

"Does it matter?" she snapped, then caught herself. "You never asked," she said, a little more calmly.

I started the car and drove down the mountain. I glanced at her and saw she was holding something in her hands. It looked like a doll.

"What's that?"

"Kira gave it to me. It was her way of apologizing for her husband. It's a matryoshka. See?" She took off the top of the doll. Inside there was a smaller wooden doll exactly like the first. She opened the second one and exposed another small doll.

"There's another one inside this," she said. "They're so Russian. Little secretive things."

Jamie threw the dolls on the seat between us, where they rolled and clattered together. We stopped at the main road. She ran a finger down the window.

"Are you okay?"

Jamie put her hand on my leg. "I guess," she said. "I feel like the little girl who found out that Santa Claus isn't real."

We drove back to town.

There was no real division in Hermitage between the Russian section and the rest. But at the first small Russian shop, the street seemed brighter, the colors of the storefronts more lively. The smells that came out of the doors were different: the rich smells of black tobacco and strong tea.

As I watched the people, I could feel what was in their minds, a collective memory filled with soldiers and police, men and women who disappeared in the night and those who died. In defense, they seemed to laugh more openly, loudly, finding in that exaggerated emotion a way of turning off the past, if only for a while.

We stopped at a gift shop. A woman with a round cheery peasant face said hello and let us browse. There were Russian records and pictures of the Kremlin and more dolls and candy and fur hats and tiny toy churches.

On one table was a stack of wooden canes, and one caught my eye. The handle of the cane was a wolf's head with a row of small white ivory teeth. The body of the wolf curved down the length of the cane.

For some obscure reason, I'd always wanted a cane, and I wanted the wolf's head. The shopkeeper came over to me, smiling.

"It's beautiful, yes?"

I nodded.

She took the cane from me. "One piece of wood," she said, running her stubby fingers down its length, "from the Ukraine."

"How much is it?"

"Seventy-five dollars," she said.

I took the cane from her and laid it on the table. Jamie walked over and picked it up.

"I'll give you sixty dollars for it," she said.

"That's too much," I said.

"Sixty dollars," Jamie said. The woman grinned. "I want to, Hunter, and it's my money. Now be quiet and take your cane."

I picked it up by the handle and felt as if I ought to be whacking servants around the Winter Palace. I was going to be hard to handle when I got back to Raven Rock.

"All I need now is a sable coat," I said.

"You look as if you need a retinue," she said and kissed me. "I feel better now. One nice thing about capitalism. It allows you to spend money when you're depressed."

42

"Will you tell me what Kharkovnakov said?"

"Thinking of beating him with your new cane?"

"Maybe." The wolf's head felt rough under my hand, and I poked at the piles of snow along the sidewalk. I caught a few people admiring it as we walked along.

"I'd advise against it," Jamie said. "He'd probably chew it to little pieces. God knows what he'd do to you."

"What did he say?"

"It was a variation on the sign at the church. I told you my Russian wasn't very good. I must be a terminal sap. I thought he'd be more like his books."

"You're not a sap," I said. "Nobody's like his books."

"Not even you?"

"Not even me."

"Boy," she said. "Today's been one big letdown after another."

"What did he say to Nicholas?"

"I didn't get very much of that either. He mentioned the ikon, but that was about it."

"He really gave it to Chernetzsky."

"The rodent?"

I laughed.

"Well," she said, laughing with me, "he looks like one, doesn't he? I didn't catch any of that, but it didn't sound good."

She put her arm through mine, and we strolled down the snow-covered sidewalk. By the time we reached the car, I had managed to transport myself back in time. We were revolutionary lovers on the lam, dashing through the Moscow streets, intent on sabotage.

Nicholas met us at the door of the church dressed in a black cassock. It changed his whole appearance. He was older, more serious, an entirely different person. He looked just like a priest.

"I'm glad you came," he said and ushered us into the church. One or two people were standing in the sanctuary. There were no pews, just a few folding chairs on either side.

Jamie hesitated.

"Please," Nicholas said when she pointed to the quote

over the door. "Don't be silly. The church can withstand one pair of slacks every now and then."

The strong smell of incense was the first thing that hit me as we entered the small, dark sanctuary. A worshiper came in after us, greeted Nicholas and crossed himself as he made his way to a wooden stand in the middle of the room. He knelt, crossing himself again, and kissed the top of the stand. He moved to the side and stood with his hands together, his mouth trembling in silent prayer.

Across the front of the church was a screen with three tiers of ikons. On either side of the screen were two small doors, and in the center was a set of double doors painted gold. Directly above the golden doors was an ikon of Christ. To his left, Mary; to his right, another figure. A pair of ikons on tall brass poles guarded both sides of the screen.

"What is all this?" Jamie whispered, and Nicholas smiled.

"You mean all that," he said and pointed to the screen. "That is called the ikonostasis. On the first row are the saint ikons. The three ikons over the doors are Christ, Mary and John the Baptist. Above them are the festival ikons. In the middle is the ikon of St. Sergius."

"Who took your pews?" I asked.

"In Russia there are no seats at all. But so many of our people are elderly that we have the chairs. Still, a lot of them stand. I've seen people standing for two and three hours," he said with great pride. "It's their faith. They don't know anything else."

Above us, a series of bells began to ring, sending three distinct tones echoing through the church.

"I have to start the service," Nicholas said. "There won't be any choir tonight. And it won't take too long." He said that directly to me. "By the way," he added, "I admire your cane. I've wanted to buy it for months."

We watched as the small church began to fill up. Most of the people were old, as Nicholas had said. They crossed themselves carefully, unbuttoned heavy coats, walked heavily to the center stand and kissed the ikon.

The bells continued. By the time they ended, the sanctuary was full, the people crowded close together, eyes resting on the ikonostasis. Some carried candles from a small table near the entrance and placed them in the memorial rack to one side. Dozens of candles flickered around the room.

The smell of the incense, the candles, the heat and the soft undercurrent of prayer—the room swarmed with images. Nicholas emerged from the golden doors at the center of the altar screen. The worshipers knelt, and we were left alone, standing outside their circle of belief.

An acolyte gave Nicholas a round brass globe filled with burning incense. The smoke trailed off the globe, writhing through the air as he waved it three times toward the congregation. He walked to the center ikon, crossed himself and kissed it. Then he continued around it and through the worshipers, crying out the words of the service in a voice that was surprisingly pure and melodic.

He circled the crowd to the back of the church. I thought he might give us some kind of sign, a recognition. But there was none. His face was locked in solemnity, and I caught a glimpse of some indecipherable fervor in his eyes. He stared straight ahead but without seeing us, as though he were searching for something beyond the walls of the church.

The service continued with an exchange of vows between priest and congregation. He sang out the liturgy in his pure voice, and the people responded in toneless, passion-filled sounds. Listening to them, watching the faces, that look of utter tranquility that came over them, I began to understand the attraction of orthodoxy, its mystery.

When the world around me came back into focus, Nicholas was finishing up the service. I looked over the room. People buttoned their coats, arranged their hats, faces shining with salvation. I saw a familiar figure.

Chernetzsky was standing next to one of the banner ikons, staring at me, his little rat face screwed up into an expression of intense hatred.

5

NICHOLAS LED US to a small local restaurant. The entrance was a wooden door in the middle of a narrow alley that ran parallel to the main street. We stepped through the door into a small foyer. To the left was an old bar, nearly hidden by thick tobacco smoke. Straight ahead, above the coat rack, was a round white clock covered with a steel grate. Over the bar was a large portrait of the general who took the jewels and ran. He was dressed in a stark white uniform, medals covering his chest. It didn't seem possible, but he appeared more arrogant than he did carved out of stone.

We stepped to the right across the unvarnished wooden floor into the dining room. Nicholas led us through the heavy tables and chairs to a row of booths in the back. The walls were covered with photographs of Russia before the deluge. Cossacks on horseback. A peasant farmer beside a wooden hut. The czar and his family boating on a placid lake. Was he thinking it would last forever?

Everyone wanted a beer, and I volunteered to get the first round. There were half a dozen men sitting at the bar. They seemed to take very little notice of me. In the far corner, high on the wall, there was a small ikon illuminated by a single candle. One of the men at the bar jerked his thumb in the direction of the ikon.

"I have my protection," he said to his friends.

One of them, a little drunker, banged his glass on the bar and held it up for all to see. "I have protection, too," he said. "Mine goes down easier." I got our beers, paid the bartender and retreated, the sound of their laughter following me out of the room.

I nearly bumped into the waitress as she was leaving our table.

"I ordered for you," Nicholas said as I handed him the bottle. "Thank you for the beer."

"What did we get?"

"A herring salad and goulash—a little spicy but very good."

"There aren't a lot of people here tonight," I said.

"I noticed," Nicholas said. "There's usually more of a crowd." He looked at his watch. "I don't understand it." He shrugged it off.

"I'm sorry about this afternoon," he said. "I've never seen him like that. He usually saves his anger for me." Nicholas smiled at Jamie. "Have you read his books?"

"Yes," she said.

"You must be a little disappointed."

"You might say that."

"He's become an angry, bitter old man," Nicholas said. "I liked him better when he was just angry."

"Kira must have a lot on her hands," Jamie said.

"Kira? She protects him. She believes in his dreams."

"To beat the world over the head with a cross?" I said.

"The world has been beaten with worse things than the cross," Nicholas said quickly, and I felt like a fool. Jamie nudged my foot under the table.

"Kharkovnakov dreams what every—or nearly every—Russian here dreams. To go back. He knows he never will, and it eats at him. He dies a little more each day," Nicholas said.

"Don't you ever want to go back?" Jamie asked.

"Go back where? I came from New York. And I don't want to go back there."

"New York?"

Nicholas smiled. "My parents were Russian, but they came here before the war. They went to New York with the rest of the immigrants." He shrugged as if to dismiss a long-remembered pain. "I'm used to living in two worlds. We were Russian—we were American. Sometimes, I'm still not sure which one I belong to."

"Are your parents still there?"

"No, they're both dead," he said.

"I'm sorry," Jamie said.

"Please," he said. "It was a long time ago. I don't go

47

back to New York very much." Nicholas was quiet for a moment.

"How did you become a priest?" I asked.

Nicholas drank his beer, and that same gaze I'd seen in the church surfaced briefly in his eyes.

"I ask myself the same question these days," he said. "I'm becoming a stereotype. The priest with doubts."

"Everyone has doubts," I said. I was just a fountain of wisdom tonight, I thought.

"True," he said as though he wanted the conversation to end, "but my doubts—I doubt the church, I doubt its survival. You've seen our congregation. How many of those people were under sixty? I don't think we have much of a future."

"No wonder you understand Kharkovnakov so well," Jamie said softly.

"You're very perceptive. May I call you Jamie?"

"Please," she said.

"When I was young," Nicholas said, "the only thing I really knew about the church was that they made you stand for hours and you couldn't go to the bathroom."

Jamie laughed and stopped herself.

"Go ahead and laugh," he said. "It is funny. My parents died when I was sixteen, and I met a young priest. He was the one who showed me that the church had meaning—what you might call an intellectual content. I didn't understand it when I was sixteen, but I was attracted to it. When I was twenty, I understood a little more. I became a priest."

"You're still a priest," I said.

"But older," Nicholas said. "I've discovered that my dreams are no different from anybody else's. I understand Kharkovnakov very well."

Our food came, and we ate in silence.

"Do you like it?" Nicholas asked.

"It's very good," I said.

When the waitress returned to clear the table, Nicholas ordered tea, Russian-style, in tall glasses.

"So, you're a writer?"

"Yes, but I'm thinking about giving it up for something serious. I might become a shepherd."

He laughed. "That's a strange aspiration."

"If you knew me well enough, it wouldn't seem strange at all."

"True," Jamie added.

"But I don't know you at all," Nicholas said. "Are you going to write about the stolen ikon?"

"I don't know. You said it wasn't stolen."

"Good point," he said. "I don't know that it has been. Someone may have been making a gesture."

"When did stealing become a gesture?"

"I forgot that you don't know much about the church. Since 1917, there has been a split in the church over leadership. There is Moscow, the mother church, and there is the American church. Some still look to Moscow, others do not. There are a great many in Hermitage who do not."

"Where do you stand?"

"I try not to make a stand. The American church received autocephaly—that's independence—only a few years ago, in 1970. The situation is delicate, and I have my instructions—accommodation."

"And Kharkovnakov doesn't go along with that."

Nicholas nodded. "He influences a lot of people who don't know what to think. That's why I do odd jobs for him and spend a great deal of my spare time arguing with him."

"And Chernetzsky?"

Nicholas' eyes narrowed. "Chernetzsky is an Old Believer."

"I've heard about them."

"Most of the stories aren't true," he said. His voice grew angry. "They're like Kharkovnakov. They live in the past. They grew up in the catacombs and that's where they want to stay, clinging to their stupidities until the earth covers them up forever."

"So, the ikon may have been taken by Chernetzsky's people—the Old Believers?"

His face lost all expression. "No, I did not say that. And I don't expect to wake up one morning to find that in some newspaper or magazine, either." He stopped for a moment. "What I'm saying is this. I think the ikon is a private af-

49

fair. Something that has no meaning for the world at large."

"Breton thinks it's valuable."

"I know what Breton thinks. He's been here before—several times. One of Fyodor's ikons—the mad monk. Did he tell you it was painted with Fyodor's own blood?"

"You never told me about that," Jamie said to me.

"Fyodor was what they called a Fool For Christ," Nicholas said to her. "He wandered the countryside speaking nonsense and ended his life in a cave, screaming at the walls. No one knows if he painted anything, let alone with his own blood."

"But it *is* an old ikon," I said. "Breton told me it might be from the twelfth or thirteenth century."

Nicholas said something in Russian that sounded extremely nasty. He crossed himself again. "He doesn't know! It is old, yes, but I've looked at it, and it isn't thirteenth-century. I know that much."

"Have other people come to look at it? Collectors?"

Nicholas threw away his answer. "A few. Not very many. We don't advertise it."

"What about the Russians?"

"The Russians? Here? I thought you understood that."

"No," I said. "Real Russians."

Nicholas burst into laughter. "Spies? You mean Dimitri, don't you? The great KGB agent. My God, Hunter, who have you been talking to about this?"

"No one in particular."

"I should hope not," he said. "Spies! Ask people about Dimitri, Hunter, they'll tell you what kind of spy he was. He was a hopeless drunk who wanted to be a big man and got in over his head. The man was a complete fool!"

"You knew him?"

"Of course I knew him. Everyone knew him. A priest died because of his stupidity."

"The one in the cemetery," Jamie said.

"Father Kyrill," Nicholas said. "He took Dimitri in, helped him, tried to keep him out of trouble. When he was arrested, Kyrill blamed himself. Six months later he was dead of a heart attack."

50

"So, you don't think the Russians would try to get the ikon back?"

"They've looted enough of our churches for ikons. They don't need to come to America to find new ones. Don't believe everything you read—or hear—from professors at Princeton."

"It must have shocked the town," Jamie said.

"It did more than that. After it made the papers"—Nicholas looked at me as if I'd been the one writing the headlines—"Hermitage closed itself off. It's taken this long for the people to feel at ease again. There were reporters everywhere—asking questions, probing, writing about it. We weren't ready for it. I would hate to see something like that happen again, just when things have started to calm down."

"If things have calmed down," I said, "then why would somebody steal an ikon from the church?"

"Hunter," Nicholas said, pleading, "I've tried to explain it. I walk a fine line here, trying to reconcile so many elements—the Old Believers, the people who are frightened and confused by the changes, the young people I have to drag into the church with tricks, Kharkovnakov—and the other people in town who look at the Russians as a sideshow that brings in the occasional tourist dollar. For you to turn what amounts to a local quarrel into something larger, something—I don't know what you want to turn it into—would do irreparable harm to my church and my community."

"I'm only interested in a story," I said and regretted it instantly. It made me wonder what in the hell I was doing.

Nicholas looked defeated.

"I can't help you anymore," he said. "This is my home. It's all I know." He looked at Jamie. "It's archaic, absolutely. Hopelessly out of step, living on dreams that died in 1917 when Lenin stood on the steps of the Winter Palace. But it's mine. The rest of the world can blow itself to hell and back and I wouldn't care."

Nicholas stood up and took Jamie's hand.

"I'm glad I met you, Jamie. I hope you keep studying Russian. It's a beautiful language. You have an ear for it." He turned to me. "I know I haven't changed your mind,

Hunter, but if you decide to write your story, I hope you'll take what I said into consideration. Don't worry about dinner, it's already taken care of." He shook my hand and left.

Jamie looked at me.

"I think it's time we went home, Hunter."

We stepped into the alley and began walking in the direction of the car. We were close to the end when two figures came around the corner and started toward us.

Chernetzsky was one of them.

I took Jamie's arm and spun her around. As I did, three more figures came out of the door of the restaurant and cut us off. I pushed Jamie against the wall, but she squirmed out from behind me. She bent down and picked up a small piece of wood. I had my cane.

"Maybe they just want to talk," she said.

"Maybe they're after my autograph."

"Hunter," she said, "I've never done this before."

"This is one helluva time to bring it up."

The five of them moved in and stood around us in a half circle. Chernetzsky saw the cane in my hand and eyed it carefully. I figured it was about five feet from the cane to the side of his head. I wanted to crack his skull and get it over with.

"The ikon," Chernetzsky said. He spoke a passable English after all.

"I don't know. Don't you have it?"

"No games," he said and spoke in Russian to the others. They started to close in on both sides.

"Where is it?" he said.

"I don't have it."

"We don't know, don't you understand?" Jamie yelled, and Chernetzsky jumped at the sound of her voice. One of the other Russians said something and laughed nervously.

I think it was George Patton who concluded that the best defense is a good offense. Maybe it was Vince Lombardi. Who the hell cared? I lashed out with the cane and smashed the nearest Russian in the middle of his face. So much for detente.

I felt his nose buckle, and blood the color of black ink sprayed out onto the snow. He fell back without a sound, holding his face.

52

Chernetzsky came at me, and I swung the cane on his arm. He yelled, and one of the Russians grabbed the cane and twisted it out of my hands. He snapped it in two and brought his fist around, clipping me on the side of my head. I dropped to one knee and drove my fist up into his crotch. It didn't seem to have the right effect. Chernetzsky yelled again and hit me on the shoulder.

Jamie threw her stick at one of the other Russians. It hit him in the chest and bounced off. He picked her up and threw her over his shoulder. She yelled and pounded on his back and he swung her around in a tight circle. I swear the son of a bitch was laughing.

The others concentrated on me. I did the most sensible thing possible and fell in a fetal position. Chernetzsky kicked me in the back. I rolled around and grabbed his foot, yanking him down. Someone tried to pull me away. I heard a voice from the other end of the alley and footsteps running toward us.

They started to back away. I saw the Russian put Jamie down on the street, but before he could get away, she reached out and slapped his face.

Nicholas said something in Russian to Chernetzsky. I let go of the little Russian's foot, and he got up quickly. Nicholas reached down to help me up.

"Are you all right?" he asked. The five thugs had stepped back against the other wall. As I straightened up, they began slipping away up the alley. Chernetzsky was the last. He stopped at the entrance, then disappeared with the rest.

Jamie threw her arms around me and squeezed. It did nothing for the incredibly sharp pain in the middle of my back. Or for the ringing in my ears.

"We're okay," I said. "Jamie?" She nodded into my chest.

"Can you walk?" Nicholas asked.

"If I can stand, I can walk," I said. Foolish me, I took a few steps, waited, then took a few more. Slowly, the three of us made it to the car.

"I began to wonder why there wasn't anybody in the restaurant," he said, "so I checked your car. When you weren't there, I came back."

"Thank you," Jamie said. "Now I want to speak to the police."

Nicholas considered her request. "I can't stop you," he said.

"But you'd prefer we didn't?"

"I don't think it would do any good."

"You don't?"

"Jamie," he said quietly, not looking at her, "at least half a dozen people will swear that Hunter started the fight with Chernetzsky."

"But you saw them!" Jamie cried.

"I saw them fighting, Jamie. I didn't see what happened before. I'm sorry. There isn't anything anyone can do."

He was right. Going to the police wouldn't do anything except add to the frustration level. Jamie stared at him in disbelief.

"I'll talk to Chernetzsky," he said. "It's the best I can do, Jamie. I really am sorry."

Jamie opened the car door. "I know you're sorry. I know you're concerned. But talking to him isn't good enough." She spoke to both of us. "I hate this kind of thing. I just hate it." She got in and shut the door. Nicholas and I stood together in the cold empty street. I still had the broken cane.

"Will you accept my apology?" he asked.

"You didn't do anything," I said. "Tell Kharkovnakov I don't have his ikon."

"Kharkovnakov?"

"Chernetzsky didn't do this on his own. We both know that. He doesn't do anything unless Kharkovnakov says it's okay."

Nicholas sounded very tired. "I don't know what's happening to these people," he said.

He was surprised when I gave him the cane. He held the two pieces apart, examining the shattered wood.

"Maybe you can get it fixed," I said.

"I'll try," he said.

When we left, he was still standing there, staring at the broken cane.

On the way home, Jamie leaned against me and said, "You're going back there, aren't you?"

"Probably."

"I'd hate to see someone like Nicholas get hurt by all this."

"He won't," I said.

"Yes, he will," she replied. "He lives here. You're just a tourist."

6

JAMIE HAS THIS marvelous little machine at her office called Lexis. It's a computer terminal and it's tied into a bigger computer somewhere and you can, at the touch of a button or two, get just about as much information on any given subject as you can handle. It's nifty and modern and costs about a zillion bucks a minute to use. Jamie nearly went crazy when I called to ask her if I could do some background checking on it.

"You absolutely can't use it during the day. Do you know how much it costs to use before five o'clock?"

"A zillion bucks?"

"More, even. Come in this afternoon. Then you can take me out to dinner. My computer, your treat. Deal?"

"How come you always want me to take you out to dinner?"

"Because I don't like to cook and I like to eat. You could take me to Paris instead. I like to do that."

"I bet you'd want to eat there, too," I said.

Jamie called me a dirty name and hung up.

I puttered around the house most of the day, adding some molding to the other room upstairs and replacing some grout around the bathtub. I heated up some veal stew and ate lunch. I started up the McCulloch and cut some wood. I tried to split some logs but gave up because of a deep pain in my back in the very same spot that Chernetzsky tried to boot into the end zone. Jules followed me around like a nurse.

I got a bottle of sake, filled the bathtub with hot water and soaked and drank for two hours. Afterward, I sat in the greenhouse and decided I wanted a red kimono with a dragon on the back. I petted my faithful companion, got dressed and drove to Jamie's office.

Jamie's firm had been doing so well she'd hired an associate, a young whippersnapper from Penn named Hangly. One of Jamie's old law professors had recommended him, and I knew why. Hangly has a brain like one of those computers I should be learning how to manipulate. A nice young man, though not terribly imaginative outside the legal cattle pen. Jamie tells me there's nobody better when it comes to putting a razor's edge on a corporate agreement. Hangly is twenty-six and knows exactly what he wants to be when he grows up. And it worries me.

Jamie says it shows my age. True. I'm afraid of people who are too certain of what they are and where they want to be in five years. They're usually the kind of people who start wars.

When I walked in a little after six, Hangly was still at his desk, looking appropriately ambitious. Plotting to take over General Motors, no doubt. I could see the visions of brilliant legal maneuvers, legions of corporate vice-presidents on their knees, begging for mercy. I probably shouldn't say things like that. He actually is a nice person. He had on his blue three-piece suit and his tie was still in place and he was more cheerful than any human being has a right to be.

"Hello, Hunter," he said. "How's life on the river?"

"It just keeps rolling along," I said and went over to the Lexis.

"Going to use the Lexis?"

"Yup." I love it when I talk like Gary Cooper.

"Do you know how much it costs?"

"A zillion bucks," I said and turned it on. I dialed in the code that Jamie had given me and plugged in the phone. The machine threw some words on the screen and I played with the keyboard until the right program came up. I punched in Kharkovnakov to start and the Lexis said that there were thirteen items where his name appeared.

I said, okay, why don't you show them to me, squirt, and the machine said that was fine and started spewing them out.

The first item told me that Kharkovnakov had been exiled from the Soviet Union for being a "parasite" and an "anti-Soviet presence." One could have worse things on one's résumé.

The next was a short article that said he had landed in New York and made a beeline for Hermitage. The article after that was a feature on Hermitage and the Russian community. It was colorful and zippy and contained no information whatsoever.

The next one, a year later, was slightly more interesting. Kharkovnakov had purchased an old abandoned hunting lodge, on the side of the mountain, that he wanted to transform into a home. He was having a little problem with the local zoning board, or at least one or two of its members.

The problem was that Kharkovankov wanted to dig down below the old foundation. The digging involved dynamite, and apparently that was going to have some kind of impact on the runoff. The board was merely concerned that Zemlya would come sliding down the mountain some warm spring afternoon and end up in the middle of Main Street.

What kind of house was he building that necessitated putting half of it underground? He wasn't saying. Eventually, he promised to reinforce the foundation, and the zoning board okayed his application.

That still didn't answer the question. The only thing I could think of was guns. Maybe Kharkovnakov was going to overthrow the Soviet Union by starting in North Jersey.

The next item was the *pièce de résistance*. Kharkovnakov was invited to give an address to the graduating class of a small upstate New York college. It turned out to be his Cross of Iron speech—at least that's what the papers called it. Privately, a number of reporters called it the 'West Eats Shit' speech, as I recall. There was some truth in both.

"The spiritual abyss into which the West has sunk can be transformed only by a spiritual fury that will sweep everything before it," Kharkovnakov told the audience, who sat on their hands in stunned silence. They probably had thought he was going to spin a bunch of cute Russian folk tales, weep profusely at America's generosity for taking him in and be gone. No such luck. Kharkovnakov beat up on them instead.

58

"Our symbol," he went on, "must be a cross. Not of wood but of molten iron. A cross that will destroy the moral deformity that has corrupted the very soul of the world. America has become a cesspool of perversion and depravity."

Half of the audience walked out, and Kharkovnakov took off, like a large bird. He threw his speech at the evacuees and started ranting at them in Russian. The one printable thing he called them was "spiritual dwarfs." After that speech, Kharkovnakov sank into his own religious bog, finished his house and didn't come out.

Rather than feeling grateful, it turned out that Kharkovnakov didn't like anybody very much—not the Russians, not the West, not even the zoning board of Hermitage.

I wanted to know where he got the money for it all.

Some of it came from the sales of his books, but that didn't seem enough to cover the kind of expenses he had incurred. I made a mental note of that and skimmed through the rest. One final short item: a where-was-the-famous-Kharkovnakov story, the kind of thing editors think up for reporters to do on slow news days. We used to call it "digging up the bodies" at the *Free Press*.

Next, I asked Lexis to find me anything on ikons. It found me several items and I read through them looking for the names of any collectors. I picked up four. One of the names appeared more often than most: Martin Angle.

The only information on Angle in the articles was that he was a wealthy businessman who had inherited a large banking fortune and made it even larger by buying one or two more banks, a handful of newspapers, an insurance company and two-fifths of Latin America. He was rich and lived in New York.

I wrote down all the names of the collectors and turned off the Lexis.

I walked across the hall to Jamie's office, sat at her secretary's desk and tried to call them. After half an hour, I found out that one had moved to Seattle, one had died, one would see me on Wednesday. Martin Angle simply wasn't available, his service said.

I was sitting at the desk when Jamie walked out and laid a piece of paper on my lap. I picked it up.

"What's this?"

"It's your bill," she said with a smirk.

I looked at the paper. My client number was 08530 and it said that I owed $321.34 to the firm.

"Not counting your phone calls and what you used on Lexis tonight," she added.

"I see."

"It's for Xeroxing and phone calls and little things like that."

"I suppose I'm just lucky to be in love with a high-priced Princeton lawyer like you."

She plucked the bill from my hands and threw it in the wastebasket. Then she sat down on my lap.

"I wanted to see your expression," she said. "It was pretty good for a second or two. What would you have done if I'd asked for a check?"

"Eaten the bill."

"Speaking of eating."

"Your place or mine?"

"Neither," she said. "Did you find anything?"

"Ever heard of Martin Angle?"

"No. I could go in my office and get *Who's Who*, but I'm really quite comfortable right where I am." I kissed her and brought my hand up under the back of her blouse. She started to bite softly on my neck.

Hangly came in to say goodnight. Jamie leaped off my lap. Hangly said something totally unintelligible, made a sharp little circle on the floor and shut the door on his way out. Jamie gave me an evil glare and went to get *Who's Who*.

"There you go," she said, handing it to me.

"Worried about your image as an employer, are you?"

She just glared at me from across the desk.

Who's Who gave Martin Angle impeccable credentials. Old Boston family into banking and shipping. The required schools: Andover, Yale undergrad, Harvard Business School. After school, a short stint in the State Department to round the boy out and to keep him away from the nastier side of public service like the U.S. Marines. Everything read like a WASP dream.

One line stood out from all the rest. Angle had done a lot

60

of traveling and had visited a lot of places on his travels. One place he'd been to quite often was the Soviet Union. He'd been there so much and done so much business with the Soviets that they gave him a medal for it.

Dinner began as a celebration, but somewhere during the evening it turned flat. I ordered a bottle of champagne and we drank a toast, but neither one of us could think of anything to say. Dinner came and we ate slowly, both of us watching the other people in the restaurant as if they had some better behavioral ideas. They all seemed to be having a good time; maybe we could learn. The champagne bobbed slowly in a bucket of melted ice.

"Something on your mind?" I asked when dinner was over.

"No," Jamie said and went through an elaborate process of laying out her napkin alongside her plate.

I sipped on my half-empty glass of champagne. It was warm.

"I feel a little funny right now," she said stiffly.

"Define the word 'funny,'" I said.

"Hunter," she said, "I want to be by myself for a while Nothing major."

I played with the bottle of champagne.

"Are you going to get angry?" she asked.

"I don't think so."

"Are you going to try to understand?"

"I always do."

"You always say you do."

"Does that mean I don't understand you every day? Or just every other Tuesday?"

"I know when you're upset," she said. "You start asking for definitions." She smiled, but it wasn't enough to change anything.

It was a good time to change the subject. The instructions appeared in large block letters: INSERT EMOTIONAL DIVERSION.

"I'm going to New York tomorrow," I said.

"What time?"

"Early," I said with a little too much emphasis.

"Hunter," she said, "the feeling never lasts very long. You know that."

"I know it doesn't," I said. I didn't tell her that I hated every minute while it did.

She kissed me good-bye and left. I ordered coffee and sat drinking it alone, trying to ignore the sounds of the people around me.

I don't think there's a more hopeless feeling in the world than sitting at an empty table, waiting to pay the check for two people.

One of whom has gone home early.

7

IT WAS TOO EARLY to go home, so I went to see Breton.

He was drunk. Or close enough to it not to make much difference one way or the other. He was also scared to death. He opened the back door cautiously, holding what appeared to be a toy hammer. He was trying to look ferocious, but he came off more like an angry Pooh, with a lumpy snarl on his soft face.

"Hunter?" he said and tried slamming the door. I stuck out my hand and stopped it. He pushed on the door and gave up, throwing the hammer down on the floor in frustration.

"Go away!" he cried. "Please just go away." Breton covered his face with his hands.

"Had a bad day?" I said, picking up the hammer. It *was* a toy, white steel and light as a piece of chalk.

"Where's Vera tonight?"

"Gone," he said vaguely. He uncovered his face. "What in God's name have you done?"

"Nothing. Where is she?"

"I don't know."

"Do you know what time she left?"

"Last night. This morning. I don't know. I got up. She wasn't here. Just, just . . ." He pointed toward the study and started to cry. The sound of his sobbing followed me as I went through the kitchen.

There was nothing wrong in the study. Except for the sharp biting odor that became nearly overpowering as I got closer to his desk. That was when I noticed the ikon.

It lay on the desk, disintegrating slowly. Someone had poured acid over it. Tiny black bubbles of paint boiled slowly on the surface. The acid had spilled over onto the desk and had eaten its way across the top of it, reducing some of Breton's papers to sludge.

Vera must have found it in the morning when she came in to cook breakfast. The message was quite clear. Whoever did it was an expert.

I heard Breton behind me.

"How could they do that?" he wailed, "Destroy something like that?"

"Did you hear anything last night? A noise, anything?"

"Noises? What kind of noises?"

"You think the tooth fairy did this? Somebody broke in here last night." Breton weaved back and forth in the doorway. "I want you to straighten up and tell me what you remember." Breton stared at me like an owl but remained standing. "Sit down!" I yelled.

He acted insulted, the jerk. He walked as correctly as possible to his chair and collapsed.

"I remember," he said thickly and stopped. "I don't remember anything. I went to sleep, got up." He pointed a trembling hand at the desk. The fact that I was there hit him again, and he yelled, "Who did you tell?"

I walked past him into the kitchen and soaked a dish towel with cold water, came back and shoved it into his face.

"You've got to stop thinking I'm one of the bad guys." Breton sputtered against the towel. "Good morning, professor."

It sobered him up a tad. He sat back in the chair and held the towel against his face. I waited.

He let it fall. "I'm sorry," he said. "I'm not a very good drunk."

"Most of us aren't. Feel up to some questions?"

"I think so."

"That's the spirit. Now, you didn't hear anything last night, right?"

"Nothing."

"You a light sleeper?"

"Yes, I suppose."

I reconsidered. Whoever had broken into the house last night was exceptionally good. I doubted it was one of the Russians.

"Now," I said, "who told you about the missing ikon?"

"I said before—someone on the phone."

"You said they were Russian."

"They spoke Russian. I don't know if they were."

"Ever hear of the Old Believers?"

"Of course."

"Ever meet any of them?"

"I don't know. I can't be sure."

"What about Vera?"

"I don't know," he cried. "What has it got to do with this?" His eyes began to look a little vague again.

"Hey!" I yelled, and shook him a little.

"I'm fine," he said. "Fine. Just woozy." He spun his finger in a loopy circle.

Terrific.

"Did Vera ever talk about them?"

"Who?"

"The Old Believers."

"Nothing. She just left." He brought both hands up like a magician. "Poof!" he said.

"What's her phone number?"

"The address book's in the desk."

I found the book and called, but there wasn't any answer. I wasn't expecting any. Vera was either hiding in the root cellar or waiting at the bus stop for a fast ride out of town. Still, I'd have to stop by her house. If she was there, maybe she would know something.

Breton was fading fast.

"Hey," I said. "Who did you tell about the ikon?"

He looked a little stricken. "No one. You, Rodger, Vera."

"Martin Angle?" I said on a hunch. The name shattered what little composure he had left.

"I don't remember."

A wink is as good as a nod.

"Did you tell him?" I asked again. "I can find out."

Breton whispered the word "yes," so softly I could barely hear him.

"When?"

"Maybe three weeks ago. I saw him at an opening. One of those things. I don't know why I went."

"How did he take the news?"

"He was totally uninterested. He said so."

"He must be a wonderful man," I said. "Was he one of the collectors you mentioned the other day?"

"Yes. There is a list on the desk."

I picked through the mess, but it wasn't there.

"It's not here."

"I wrote it down. I don't know. I want to go to bed," Breton said.

"In a minute. Give me the names." He told me the same names I'd found through the computer. "Now tell me about Angle."

"He's rich."

"I know he's rich. I want to know what he does with the Russians."

"He's an Armand Hammer type—does a lot of business with them. He's got a nice collection. He buys and buys and buys. That's what he does. Doesn't care. Just buys and buys."

"What else?"

Breton's head sagged to his chest. He really was a bad drunk.

There was a cop car parked out in front of Vera's when I arrived. I went to her door and knocked. No one answered. The cop rolled down his window and told me to step over to the car.

"Yes?" I said. Heat blew through the window into my face. For once, I wanted a cop to tell me to get in the car. He didn't.

"She's not home" he said.

"What happened?"

He was good-naturedly suspicious. "Why do you care?"

"I just talked to Professor Breton. She's his house-keeper."

"Why didn't the professor make it?" he said.

I made a motion like raising a glass. "He's a little under the weather at the moment."

"So's his housekeeper. Neighbor found her on the bed-room floor."

"Is she alive?"

"Barely," he said. "I went in with the ambulance guys.

66

They said it was stroke. Whole left side paralyzed. Sargeant told me to stick around and see if anyone showed up." He looked me up and down. "And here you are."

"I'm not all that interesting."

"Let's see some ID," he said.

He looked over my license. "We tried calling Breton, but nobody answered. How come he got plastered?"

"Don't they all?"

"I thought most of them were on drugs," he said.

"Did she say anything?"

"Who, the housekeeper? No."

"Breton wanted to know if she was all right."

"I don't know. She had her bags half packed when she keeled over. That's what it looked like, anyway. Stuff was scattered all over the place." He whistled softly. "Old people, Jesus. I hope I die before I get that old."

"Pete Townshend said the same thing."

"Who?"

"That's the one," I said and left.

I sat around my house and got depressed. I could see Vera coming into Breton's house in the morning and smelling the acid. She probably knew the house better than her own, and it must have frightened her half to death. She would have left right away, rushing home, scared of every shadow, every noise. Throwing her clothes into her suitcase, tearing things out of the drawers. Then, nothing. A sharp pain in her head, a flutter of confusion. Whatever she knew or might have seen was sealed off, perhaps forever.

The phone rang. It was Jamie. I tried sounding more cheerful than I felt.

"Where were you?" she asked.

"I was out looking for a cheap floozie."

"Any luck?"

"No," I said. "They all went home early."

She was quiet. "I wish I were there with you," she said.

"I wish you were, too."

"You sound a little angry," she said.

"I'm not," I said. "Just a little depressed." I didn't tell her why.

"Are you coming home tomorrow night?"

"Probably."

"Will you cheer up?"

"Eventually."

"You shouldn't be that depressed," she said. "The good guys won the fight. We're the good guys, remember."

The good guys. I wondered if it would make Vera happy to know how well the battle was going.

8

I GOT UP at five and left Jules howling in the dark to catch the antiquated two-car trolley called the Dinky from Princeton out to the Junction. I stood on the platform with fifty other lost souls who were forced by circumstances, American Express and sadistic interest rates to go through this pernicious ritual every day.

I got on the train and sat next to a man in a three-piece suit who was reading the stock tables in the *Journal*. I noticed that he kept whimpering as he turned the pages. Just one more bad week on the Big Board. I could see Nantucket fading rapidly as the big family resort this year.

I'm something of a hypocrite in this and I know it. I'm sure whoever handles my money worries about these things. I worry about the price of firewood and I dressed the part. I had on my best Levi's, boots and a terrific-looking black wool turtleneck; the outfit brings out my Alain Delon tendencies. Whenever I wear it, I want to sit in corner cafes and make rude and pointless remarks to the waitress. After all that, my sheepskin coat was just icing on the cake.

The train pulled underneath the Hudson and rolled into Penn Station. I cut my way through the crowd to Seventh Avenue, grabbed a taxi and headed uptown to see the other New York collector on my list, a man named Arnold Haddonford. He had told me on the phone that he thought it would be interesting to talk to someone who actually *lived* in New Jersey.

Arnold Haddonford was a nice old gentleman of highly independent means who rode around his apartment in a wheelchair and employed a large human named Conrad to watch over him. They lived in one of those buildings on Park Avenue whose landlords don't give out their list of occupants to anyone except the IRS and then only after a long court battle. Haddonford apologized for not getting up to greet me.

"Terrible legs," he said when I took a seat in the living room. "Soon I'll have to have Conrad compile an index of the things that have given out on me."

For a man compiling a laundry list of afflictions, he seemed healthy enough. It was probably the soothing effect of all that money, I thought. His thin face was shiny pink, and the fringe of white hair that surrounded his freckled bald head made him appear maddeningly robust, not at all like a man waiting around for the next bit of medical bad news. Even in the chair, he was something of a dandy: a double-breasted blue blazer, bright-yellow shirt, dark-gray trousers and a snappy-looking red-and-white polka-dot ascot which added just the right "accent."

"You said you were interested in my ikons," he said. "I'm afraid I've loaned them all out. Museums, that sort of thing. I've collected a great many things in my lifetime, including three wives who loved me dearly. It cost me a considerable amount of money to extricate myself from their love. Art, I've found, is substantially less taxing."

"The ikons?" I said.

Haddonford looked dismayed. "For an apparently intelligent young man, your conversation lacks diversity. Would you like a glass of wine?"

"No thanks. The last time I started drinking this early, I ended up crawling around in a ditch on all fours. I haven't even had a second cup of coffee yet."

"That's easily remedied." Haddenford pressed a button on the arm of his chair, and Conrad appeared at the other end of the room.

"Yes?"

"Bring us some coffee and something to eat. I'll have my usual."

His usual turned out to be a bottle of burgundy and a poached egg. I survived on coffee and some very good pastry.

"Now," he said, finishing one glass and pouring another, "you're interested in ikons. To purchase?"

"No, I'm interested in one particular ikon—part of the Fyodor set."

70

"The Fyodor set? What do you know about them?"

I told him what I knew. He listened carefully.

"That has always struck me as an appalling load of rubbish, wouldn't you say?"

"I haven't the faintest idea."

"Ikons painted with blood? Rubbish!" he said. "If you believe that, you aren't half as intelligent as you appear."

"People accuse me of that all the time. I've learned to live with it."

He laughed. "Who else are you seeing on this investigation? That's what it is, isn't it? Are you a detective or something?"

"I'm a writer."

"A writer. Isn't that interesting. Who else are you seeing?"

"Martin Angle."

Haddonford's pink face got a little pinker, and he wheeled away from the table. When he got to the window, he spun around, chewing on his bottom lip in a rather elegant fury.

"That man," he started to say and bit his lip again. "Did he send you here?"

"I've never met him."

"I didn't ask you that. Did he hire you to harrass me?"

"Mr. Haddonford, I don't work for Martin Angle. I came here to talk about ikons for a story I'm working on."

"Can you prove that statement?"

"Call up my editor."

He hit the button on the chair again, and Conrad stuck his upper torso through the door. Haddonford spoke to me. "Give Conrad the information."

Conrad took the number and went into the other room. A few minutes later, he emerged and announced that I was okay.

"A man named Rodger Jones said that Mr. Hunter was looking into a story for the *Times*. He also said we should hide any valuables we might have because Mr. Hunter was a well-known kleptomaniac," Conrad said in an extremely unamused voice.

Haddonford managed a smile. "Fine, Conrad, thank

you." Conrad vanished again. "Your editor seems to have a sense of humor."

"I hope it turns rabid and bites him."

"Humor is one of those things that might save us all. It's in very short supply."

"Does Angle have any to spare?"

"Martin Angle is a man without much of a sense of humor," he said. "Let me show you something."

He drove his wheelchair over to a large cabinet, opened it and took out a photo album. He pointed to a picture of a statue, a woman holding a bow and arrow.

"That is a statue of Diana. It was sculpted in Greece sometime around 450 B.C. It once belonged to me. I keep the picture as a reminder."

"A reminder of what?"

"That Martin Angle had it destroyed."

Haddonford sipped his wine. "I've never been a violent man, but I seriously considered having him killed because of what he did."

"Half of Manhattan gets that urge waiting for a taxi. I've had it myself."

"Have you? I've never been comfortable with it. My money has given me access to certain options that most people only dream about. I think perhaps it's better that way."

"Did someone kill your statue?"

"In a way yes. I purchased it on an overseas trip. This was nearly ten years ago. I was a friend of the man who sold it to me, and he honored my offer, although Angle made him a substantially better one. I was very much the gentleman about it. I even suggested that perhaps Angle might wish to display it in a gallery he had an interest in at the time."

Haddonford downed half the glass of wine in one gulp.

"I underestimated the man," he said. "During shipment, someone smashed the statue beyond repair. At least that's what my investigators said. They never found out who did it—or who had it done. But it was Angle. He is cold-blooded and vicious, with no sense of responsibility toward anyone but himself."

"Now I know that when I invite him to tea I'll have to

hide the good china, but that doesn't tell me anything. The world is filled with nasty people. But most of them don't get to spend weekends in Moscow very often."

"Martin Angle *has* only one dimension as far as I'm concerned. He is a *collector*, and I use that term with disdain. He acquires things simply to acquire them. Ownership without appreciation, possession without love. It's a sickness that often comes with great wealth. He buys things so he can deprive the rest of the world of their beauty. That is his sole motivation."

"If I show up at his front door uninvited, will he talk to me or have me shot?"

"Possibly both. If he's in the city and if he thinks he might benefit somehow, he may talk to you. But don't expect very much from him. And be prepared to duck. What is this story you're writing, anyway?"

I told him.

"It sounds like Angle. He has a long reach and he's very careful. I can guarantee you won't get a thing out of him. You'll have to find out who's working for him. Then, possibly, you might find your missing ikon."

"I'm curious about Angle's relationship with the Russians. What exactly does someone like Angle sell to them?"

"Toothbrushes, for one. The Russians love American toothbrushes. Beyond that, I know very little except that he's quite chummy with the leadership over there and he seems to have little trouble with our own people in Washington. Never a problem there, I can assure you."

"I don't suppose there's anything more to it. Could he be slipping the odd microchip in with the dental floss? Or—"

Haddonford cut me off. "I've thought about whether Angle could be doing more than trading with the Russians. I frankly don't know. If he is working with them, it would be out of greed. He's a greedy man—with powerful friends. Do you know James Enderson?"

"*The* James Enderson? The Secretary of State? He hardly ever calls anymore."

"The *late* Secretary of State," Haddonford said dryly. "He was close to Angle's father and got him his first job. Helped him with the Kremlin as well. Angle has been surrounded with important people throughout his life. You're treading on dangerous waters."

"It's beginning to look that way."

"You may need some help," he said. "I have time on my hands and a certain amount of influence. Conrad might come in handy as well."

"I'm not sure I can afford your help, Arnold. Your price may be a tad high for me."

"I wasn't planning on charging you by the hour," he said.

"I didn't mean that. It was more along the lines of the free-lunch theory."

"I see. I would like to be kept informed, that's all. Is that too high for you?"

"Maybe," I said. "If you're expecting a regular update. I'm reliable but not that reliable. I may get busy."

Haddonford took a card out of his coat pocket and wrote something on the back. "That is my private number. If you need anything, call me. I'll speak to Conrad. He was a Rhodes scholar, you know."

"That devil," I said. "He looks like a thug with taste."

"Golden Gloves champion, twice," Haddonford said. "I enjoy people who can carry on an intelligent conversation as well as other things." He looked at my face. "Tell me, how did you get that bruise on your face?"

"A lull in the conversation," I said.

"What an interesting life you must lead, Mr. Hunter."

"I never looked at it like that. I always thought of it as sort of dull and uneventful. A victim of circumstance."

"If you upset Martin Angle, it will cease to be dull." He wheeled over next to me. "There isn't a day that passes that I don't look at that picture. My anger hasn't diminished in eleven years. Use my name when you see him. He'll rise to that bait, I think."

He saw me to the door.

"Give him my best," he said. "Tell him I think about him often."

9

MARTIN ANGLE owned two adjoining buildings near Sutton Place, on the same street where they busted a very expensive brothel several years back. That was the one where Xaviera Hollander made her reputation driving rich old men crazy with Cream of Wheat enemas or whatever she did to them.

The doorman sat in one of the buildings like a retired Bavarian general waiting to teach the low countries another lesson in servility. He let me in and asked me what I wanted. I told him and checked my hair in the shine of his brass buttons. It seemed to annoy him immensely.

"Do you have an appointment?"

"No," I said. "I'm very spontaneous."

"I thought you said you were a writer."

"That, too."

"I'll see if he's available. Your name is Hudson?"

"Hunter."

"And you're with the *Times?*"

"With it but not of it."

"Take a seat." He made obsequious noises into the phone and gave me one of those you - could - die - and - go - to - heaven - before - you - get - what - you - want - out - of - me - you - pathetic - shithead smiles.

"Mr. Angle is occupied right now," he said, hanging up the receiver.

"What a shame," I said. "Would you tell him that I just came from Arnold Haddonford's and he asked me to extend his best wishes. Perhaps Mr. Angle will see me then."

The doorman conveyed my message. To everyone's surprise, I was allowed to enter, which confused the doorman all to hell. It's a tough act to be rude and civil at the same time, but bless his pointed little head, he pulled it off. I got in the elevator and rode it up to the fifth floor.

A young man in a dark-blue suit who was as clean-cut as a member of the Mormon Tabernacle Choir met me at the elevator and walked through several hallways before he ushered me into a large room that appeared to be a library.

On the far wall was an expanse of drapes. To my right was a fireplace with several carefully set logs burning exquisitely. In front of the fireplace were three expensive-looking leather chairs and a coffee table with a vase of fresh flowers in the middle. Over the fireplace was an English landscape that looked like a Turner.

The other two walls were filled with books. In front of the far wall was the largest desk I'd ever seen in my life. Seated at the desk, in a chair with high winged sides, fingers pressed together like the reflection of a spider on a mirror, sat Martin Angle.

I had the feeling he expected me to come to him. Instead, I went over to the painting above the fireplace. "Golly," I said. "It is a Turner."

"If you knew anything at all about painting, you wouldn't need to inspect it. Haddonford should have told you that about me," Angle said. His voice was patrician in the extreme.

"He said you were a collector. He used the term disdainfully." Angle stared down his thin elegant nose at me. "He also implied that you steal from widows and orphans."

"But only at Christmas, I suppose," Angle said.

"Especially."

Angle appeared bored. "I collect the best," he said. "I have no use for anything else. That separates me from people like Arnold Haddonford."

"And when you can't have the best?"

He laughed quietly. "I try to accept the situation like a gentleman."

"He told me you haven't done so well in that area."

Angle moved a little farther into the light. I noticed that the skin on his cheeks was pulled tight, as if something had a grip on the back of his scalp. His hair was combed down across a large forehead in short clipped bangs, a style favored by several Roman emperors. Martin Angle looked as if he still needed a few Christians to toss around.

"Arnold Haddonford is an annoying old man," he said. "And you're becoming an irritation." I walked across an acre and a half of Oriental rug to get to the desk. Martin Angle managed to look down at me from the depths of his chair. "I don't waste time on fools. I pay other people to do that. You now have thirty seconds to convince me you're not a fool."

"That's a tough one," I said. "Why did you steal the Fyodor ikon from St. Sergius'?" Angle's hands spread out slowly across the desk, spiders looking for a home. "How am I doing so far?"

"Did Haddonford accuse me of taking this ikon?"

"He said it was something you might do if you felt the urge."

"Do you really think a man in my position has to steal to satisfy his urges?"

"Depends on the urges."

Angle sat back in his chair, silent, brooding.

"Arnold said you were a man who bought things so you could deprive the world of their beauty," I said. "It's only a short hop from there to stealing."

"I could have you thrown out," Angle said.

"If this were Paraguay, you could have me tortured and shot. But if you threw me out now, I'd think you were hiding something and I'd come back."

His hands found each other again. They coupled with an exquisite slowness.

"What a terrifying thought," he said. "Why couldn't Arnold Haddonford have taken it?"

"He's an old man in a wheelchair."

"Old men in wheelchairs are as dangerous as anyone else. More so, in fact. They have to prove it. Look at Franklin Roosevelt. Besides, Haddonford has help."

"Conrad's a Boy Scout."

"I suppose he trotted out that old story about the statue?"

"He said you hired somebody with a hammer to turn it into gravel."

"So it must be true, of course," he said. "What if I told

you that the seller changed his mind at the last minute and sold it to me? Does it occur to you that Haddonford might have smashed the statue himself to keep me from taking possession of it the minute it arrived in New York?"

"I'll ask him."

"And he'll deny it. You don't know how much he hates me."

"I've got an idea."

"No," he said, "you do *not*."

There was a chair in front of the desk. I sat down and waited.

"Why would I do something as bizarre as stealing an ikon?" he asked.

"Because you wanted it."

"I could buy it."

"I don't think they'd sell it. A man in your position isn't used to being turned down."

"If you're so certain, you should be talking to the police, not to me."

"Not yet. Did you know it was stolen before Professor Breton told you about it?"

"Ah," Angle said, "the good professor. Did I do something to him as well?"

"Someone did."

"You have a number of irritating suspicions—stealing ikons, threatening professors—or did I murder him in his sleep?"

"Are you a Russian spy?"

Angle flushed and broke into a laugh. For some odd reason I started laughing with him.

"If I were a spy," he said, "I'd be one for our side. We could use a few decent ones, don't you think?"

He took a cigarette out of the case on his desk and lit it.

"I don't care which side wins anymore. There aren't any *sides*, just two opposing groups with flags of convenience so they can justify their own existence. I am constantly amazed at their ingenuity. Here."

Angle spun around in his chair and pulled two objects down from one of the shelves behind him. He sat them on

78

the desk. They were a pair of medals. "Do you see any significant difference between them?"

They were remarkably similar. One had an engraved head of Lenin on it, the other a picture of George Washington.

"That should tell you something about the nature of modern governments," Angle said, putting them back on the shelf. "They all find it necessary to subscribe to some fantasy. The Russians think they were chosen by history. We think we were chosen by God. You could put all the bureaucrats in one room and unless they opened their mouths, you wouldn't be able to tell them apart."

"Ours dress better," I said.

"Because they're paid more than they're worth."

"How much are you worth?"

"I can buy anything I want," he said. "I don't have to steal anything. I could even buy you. Perhaps not with money. I suspect you're the type of person who dislikes wealth."

"I don't dislike wealth, I dislike what some people do with it," I said. "And I'm not for sale."

"People will sell almost anything in the world," he said, rising from the desk. "I'll show you."

We left the library and passed the Mormon, who was sitting diligently at a desk in the small room across from the library.

"Tell her to wait for me," Angle said. "I'll only be a minute." He walked very quickly, taking long strides, to the end of the hallway and pushed his way through a set of double doors.

The doors opened onto a forest.

The forest grew up from the center of the other building. I looked down through half a dozen full-sized trees. Overhead was a large glass dome, and sunlight shone down into the building, breaking delicately through the trees. Below me, I heard the soft gurgle of the stream that ran through the middle of it all.

I stood at the railing and looked down into the center of the forest. There, in the middle of it, stood the Diana statue. The sunlight caught the white stone and made the figure come alive. Angle spoke behind me.

"It's a copy," he said. "I had it made when I heard that the real one had been lost."

I looked around me. Surrounding the forest was a wide runway that flowed in a circle along the sides of the building from the first floor to where we stood at the top. On the walls was Angle's art collection. I could see some of it: a row of glass cases that contained what appeared to be Chinese porcelain vases; a pair of French hunting tapestries; two suits of armor; some Impressionist paintings. It was Angle's private museum. It seemed to have been put together without any sense of rhythm or proportion. Except, maybe, greed.

"Turn around," he said. Behind us was a row of ikons.

"I like dealing in facts," Angle said. "This is a fact. This is what money can buy."

I approached one of the ikons, a portrait of three saints with a brilliant scarlet background.

"I bought that in Moscow," Angle said. "Even the Soviets are forced to buy and sell in the marketplace, just like the capitalists."

"How old is it?"

"I was told it was fifteenth-century," he said. "I have someone to authenticate them for me. How much do you know about ikons?"

"Not very much."

"But you know about the one in Hermitage."

"I was there yesterday."

"Were you?" he said. "Did you meet the great man?"

"Kharkovnakov? Yes."

"One of the lucky few," he said. "Then you know what a lunatic he is. If anyone took the ikon, it would be Kharkovnakov and his band of fools."

"I thought he was still pretty influential in the church."

"As a political force, the church is dead," he said. "Kharkovnakov is just another relic. Stealing an ikon would be typical—a useless act of revenge."

"What would you do? As a political act."

"For revenge," Angle said and smiled, "I would have blown up the church and the ikon with it."

"That seems a bit extreme."

"That depends entirely on your point of view. Certainly

no more extreme than stealing an ikon that I have little or no interest in owning. Do you still think I took it?"

"Just between you and me," I said, "I think you're crazier than batshit."

Angle stepped toward me, his hands doubling into fists. I waited for him to try to hit me. At the last moment, he turned quickly and walked past me to the door.

"Is your tour over?" I said.

Angle had disappeared, but the Mormon was standing in the hall, waiting for me. His face was a little flushed and I could see he'd worked himself up into a polite frenzy; he looked as if he was ready to cloud up and rain all over me. He took my arm and began pulling me toward the elevator. I let him do that for a few feet before I stopped.

"I wasn't ready to leave yet," I said.

He reached inside his coat and pulled out a small silver revolver. I raised my hands slightly.

"My God," I said, pointing suddenly to a spot on the wall near his head.

He looked away and I grabbed the gun, twisting his wrist hard enough to hurt. The Mormon let go of it, yelped and banged into the wall.

"You should have stayed in bed today," I said.

"Oh, shit," the Mormon said, shaking his head.

"Remember Kurt Vonnegut's advice," I told him. "You are who you pretend to be, so be very careful who you pretend to be. You thought you were Jimmy Cagney but you're really Pat O'Brien."

I emptied the bullets in my hand.

"So," I said, "what's it like working for a lunatic?"

"It has its moments," he said, looking at the gun in my hand.

"This isn't one of them." I pointed toward a closet near the elevator. "Out of harm's way," I said.

He got inside. "Beats a poke in the eye with a sharp stick," I said.

He didn't seem amused.

I found the library and listened by the door. A woman's voice said, "I can't deal with this anymore, Martin."

"I'm not interested in your problems," Angle said.

"He wants to know what happened to it," she said.

"Then tell him!" Angle shouted.

They stopped talking for a moment, then the woman said, "I could go back to Rome."

"Kimberly," Angle said, laughing, "let's be realistic, shall we? They'd arrest you."

I opened the door and stepped inside. Standing by the desk was a thin blond woman in black slacks and a black top. She had a small pixie face, and she didn't smile at me.

"What are you doing here?" Angle said.

"Just hanging out. Pretend I'm not here."

"Who is this person?" Kimberly said.

"Think of me as a ship in the night," I said and tossed the gun on the rug in front of her. "Thought you might want this." She looked at it blankly; she was probably used to guns landing at her feet, maybe it was commonplace in Rome. She raised her head. One corner of her mouth lifted in a smile.

"You're a very stupid man, Hunter," Angle said.

"If you keep saying things like that, I'm going to get angry." I smiled at Kimberly. "You come here often?"

Angle shook like an attack dog that's been kept on a chain too long. He just sat there and twitched.

"Look at him," I said. "How can you stand it, honey?"

Angle snapped. He came around the desk and picked up the gun. Kimberly backed away. Without hesitating, he aimed it at me and fired. The gun went click-click-click.

I grinned and dropped the bullets on the rug. "You are crazier than batshit," I said and waved good-bye. In ten seconds or so, Angle was going to reload the gun. I didn't want to be around for that.

I let the Mormon out of the closet and got in the elevator.

"He's not in a good mood," I said. The Mormon looked as if he wanted to jump in the elevator with me. The doors began to close.

I walked until I found a bar. I ordered a shot of whiskey, slammed it down and ordered an Irish coffee to go.

"This look like a 7-11 to you?" the bartender said. He had bloodshot eyes and a day's worth of stubble on his face.

"You look like you'd do anything for a ten-dollar bill." I slid one on the counter.

"I should tell you where to stack your empties."

"Probably," I said. He crumpled the ten in his hand, glancing once around the bar before he did it.

"It's an off night," he said. The ten disappeared in his pocket.

"Looks that way."

"Bar whiskey all right?"

"Wouldn't have it any other way," I said.

Irish coffee in hand, I walked back to Angle's and waited near the corner of the building across the street. I waited there for two hours. In that time, I worked out an entire disarmament agreement, accepted the Nobel Prize, wrote a smash Broadway play and was named editor of a major metropolitan newspaper. In between all that, I froze my ass off.

At five o'clock, Kimberly came out of Angle's alone. A cab was waiting for her. There wasn't another cab in sight. I ran after her for about six blocks until the cab took a sharp left. I stood on the corner and watched as it roared through a yellow light and was gone. I found a phone booth and called Rodger. I was lucky. He was working late.

"I'm busy," Rodger said.

"I don't want to hear about it. I'm cold and hungry and I need a place to stay."

"You have a home," he said.

"I'm in New York, Rodger."

"Oh."

"Was that the warmth of human kindness in your voice or are you just glad to hear from me?"

"What do you need, Hunter?"

"I just told you. I need a place to stay."

"I don't have the room," he said.

"Then give me some money, so I can rent a room for the night so I can keep checking out your goddam story."

"I can't authorize too much. How about fifty dollars?"

"How about I walk over to the *Times* and eat your face?"

"A hundred. That's the best I can do."

"Tell me where I can use it."

He gave me the name of a midtown hotel where I could charge a room to the paper. As an afterthought, he asked, "How's it going?"

"It's going fine, Rodger. I really think there's a story here. In fact, I think there's such a good story here I'm going to sell the son of a bitch to Rupert Murdoch just to teach you some manners."

"You wouldn't do that to me, Hunter. Would you?"

"Rodger," I said, "do you read lips?"

Out of sheer spite, I walked to the hotel. My room turned out to be all white and only slightly larger than my bathroom. But the shower worked and the food in the restaurant was warm and harmless. After dinner, I called Arnold Haddonford.

Conrad answered the phone.

"This is Hunter. Can I talk to him?"

Arnold was on the line almost immediately.

"I take it you saw our mutual friend?" he said.

"I don't think he likes either one of us."

"We'll just have to live with our disappointment."

"I need some help, Arnold."

"So soon?"

"First I need a car. I don't know for how long."

"I'll have Conrad bring the Mercedes around."

"I don't *need* a Mercedes."

"It's the only one I have," he said. "Anything else?"

"Some information."

"Yes?"

"Do you know a woman named Kimberly? Tall, very blond?"

Haddonford paused, and the pause turned into a silence large enough to drive a truck through.

"Hello?" I said.

"Yes," he answered, "I know her."

"Who is she?"

"Where did you see her?"

"She was with Angle."

"Is she what you want the car for?"

"Yes."

"This isn't something I want to discuss over the phone."

"I'll be there in about fifteen minutes."

"We'll hold our breaths until you arrive, I'm sure," he said.

* * *

"Her name is Kimberly Wyeth," Arnold said. "Do you remember my mentioning James Enderson?"

"The Secretary of State?"

"The *late* Secretary," he said sourly. "Kimberly is his stepdaughter."

"Why doesn't she use his name?"

"How should I know?" Arnold said, throwing up his hands. "I suppose she's very modern and all that. Prefers her own name. Don't all modern women have trouble with their names these days?"

"Not the ones that I know."

Arnold's hands fluttered to rest on his knees. "Before I go any further," he said, "I want to know what you intend to do."

"You know where she lives?"

"I do."

"Good. I'm going to stake her out."

"I beg your pardon."

"I'm going to watch her and see what she does. If I'm lucky she won't see me while I'm doing it."

"Oh, stake her out. Is that detective talk? It sounds rather dull. Why would you want to do that?"

"Because I can't do it to Angle and I think she's involved. How, I don't know. Let's call it a hunch. Besides, I don't have anything else."

"I don't think it will amount to much," he said. Arnold was trying to act uninterested and not doing very well. "Do you really think she's involved?"

"It's worth a wasted evening," I said. "How well do you know her?"

"We've met," he said, fussing with one of the buttons on his coat.

I sat on the couch and picked up a magazine. "When you're ready to tell me about her, Arnold, you let me know."

He looked up at me angrily, but it passed.

"I suppose it is a little obvious, isn't it?"

"I'm afraid so, Arnold."

"Then I ought to tell you about Kimberly Wyeth," he said. "It isn't what you think."

"It never is, Arnold."

"I met her in Zurich, several years ago," he said. "We were both interested in the same artist. Naturally, we had dinner together. I found her very charming. This was before I knew precisely who she was."

He took a sip of wine and smiled sadly.

"As I said, she was very charming, but beneath all that charm there was a very confused, very troubled young woman. I made a point of finding out more about her."

He looked at me sharply, aniticipating some kind of rebuke. "It was the prerogative of a gentleman," he said.

Kimberly Wyeth, Haddonford discovered, had a normal expensive upbringing. Undergraduate work at Smith, then two years in Paris at the Sorbonne while her stepfather was telling the French how to run their country from the vantage point of the U.S. embassy. Her real father had divorced her mother when Kimberly was still a child and now lived somewhere in South Africa.

Kimberly modeled a bit in Paris and fell in with the usual crowd, various crown princes and the kind of people who blew silver dollars out their nose when they sneezed.

"Embassy life can be rather boring for a young woman as intelligent as Kimberly," Haddonford said.

"She got in trouble," I suggested.

"Yes," he said, "I'm afraid so."

She had one or two shoddy and well publicized affairs before things got sticky. Her stepfather, keeping one eye on his charge and another on his career, sent her to Switzerland, where she stayed for six months before running off to Rome. In Rome, she drank, drove several expensive automobiles into trees and screwed anything that walked, crawled or had been dead for less than three days. In between times, she snorted her way through the Roman low life and eventually got arrested for keeping several ounces of cocaine in her purse just in case she got edgy.

At which point, her stepfather plucked her out of the muck and dragged her off to Moscow on his way up the State Department ladder. When he made it back to Washington as Secretary, she returned to that city's somnambulant life-style without a peep.

"She opened a gallery in Georgetown," Arnold said. "She did very well, kept her own name but people knew who she was just the same. Who wouldn't want to buy a nice little two-thousand-dollar print from the stepdaughter of the American Secretary of State? She sold mostly to the Arabs, I understand."

"Sounds right."

"I saw her several months ago, here, at a gallery I know. She seemed quite happy."

"Maybe she still is, Arnold."

"Not if she's seeing Martin Angle. He's using her, the way he uses everyone." He paused. "I'd like you to make sure she doesn't get hurt!" he snapped.

"I may not be able to do that," I said.

Arnold sulked, trying to hide it by drinking more wine.

"Perhaps it's only my vanity," he said, "but I tried to help her once. I *did* help her, I thought. Perhaps I'm just upset to discover I had no influence on her whatsoever."

"Maybe there's nothing to it," I said. "I could be wrong."

"Yes, you *could* be," he said and swore to himself. "I'm sorry. If she's involved with Martin Angle, there's something there. I just hope it isn't serious."

"I'll do what I can, Arnold."

"I know you will. I suppose that's all I've a right to ask for," he said, but not very convincingly.

The car was a Mercedes 450 SLC. Conrad took me over to the garage and explained it all to me.

"Do you like Chopin?" he said, punching a tape into the deck.

"I don't mind it. Mostly I listen to rock and roll."

Conrad made a face. "I've never understood rock music," he said.

"There isn't much to understand, Conrad. It's loud and it drives you insane. If you play it loud enough, it kills all your houseplants."

"And that's why you like it?" He seemed positively appalled.

I got in the car and started it up.

"Tell me, Conrad, is Arnold in love with Kimberly Wyeth?"

The question took him by surprise.
"I'm sure I wouldn't know," he said.
"Would you tell me if you did?"
Conrad smiled. "Absolutely not."

10

I DROVE TO Manhattan Towers, an imposing apartment complex near midtown, and waited for Kimberly Wyeth to do something.

I had exhausted Chopin and was moving deeply into Mozart when Kimberly Wyeth came out of the front entrance of the Towers in a full-length leather coat and acting as if she was in a hurry. She waited by the curb but didn't make conversation with the doorman next to her. A silver-blue BMW pulled in front of her. She ignored the man who held the car door open for her, got in and drove off. Kimberly did not tip the help.

She drove carefully through the traffic. I stayed on her blind side, always a car or two away. The car handled beautifully. When it was all over, I knew what I was going to do. I was going to ask Arnold to buy me a Mercedes for my very own.

Kimberly drove through midtown and then cut left toward the river. She went directly to the warehouse district off Tenth, a few blocks up from the car pound. I pulled over to the curb, turned off my lights and watched her car move swiftly away. Six blocks down, she turned into one of the warehouses. With my lights still off, I drove halfway there, parked and got out.

It was colder near the river, and the wind whistled through the buildings. A cat ran across the street ahead of me, stopped, then dashed for the darkness on the other side.

I came up to the corner of a building and peered around the edge. Kimberly's car was parked next to a small black sedan in the middle of the empty lot. A single spotlight from one of the loading docks shone down between the two cars.

Kimberly was standing next to the sedan, talking to a man in a heavy black overcoat. The wind picked up their voices and carried them back to me. They were speaking Russian. The man spoke loudly, in a sullen, petulant voice. He waved his arms up and down. He was clearly upset over something.

Kimberly stepped back and slapped him across the face. The man staggered against the car and started for her. She said something sharp and he stopped, spitting on the ground in front of her. Kimberly didn't move. The man gave up. He opened the back door of the sedan and took out a small aluminum suitcase and dropped it between them. Kimberly reached in her pocket and handed him an envelope. She picked up the suitcase and went around to her car while he stood watching her. He said something, but she didn't respond. She didn't even bother to look at him.

The BMW spun around in the lot, and I took off, throwing myself into a doorway as her headlights flashed into the street. She checked the street and turned in the opposite direction. I watched her taillights fade and ran for my car. The Russian in the sedan pulled out after her as I got inside.

I decided the Russian deserved special attention and followed him. After all, he was the one with diplomatic plates.

I tailed him back to midtown and then, oddly, into Times Square. He circled around and pulled into a garage near Tenth Avenue. I drove right in after him, and waited while he gave his car to the attendant.

I sat in my car and watched him leave the garage. He was medium height, medium weight and medium build, with a soft face and a thin little mustache to go with it. He definitely looked like a Boris to me. He walked past my car, keeping his head down. The only thing out of the ordinary about him was the small leather case he carried in one hand. He walked out of the garage and turned left. I tossed my keys to another valet and hurried to catch up to Boris. He was already a block up the street, heading into Times Square. I kept that distance and followed along behind him as if I knew what I was doing.

For half an hour, Boris pretended to look at Japanese radios bigger than his head. He stayed on Broadway and covered both sides, gazing at the windows and standing behind the crowds around the three-card monte dealers, who never let cold weather keep them from their appointed rounds. Finally, he headed up 42nd to Eighth. In the middle of the block, he walked into a place called Adult Delights.

Boris was into sleaze.

The place was swell. You came in off the street into a never-never land of blue lights and men who would not look at one another. They all drifted between the "gift shop" and the peep shows. In the "gift shop" you could buy anything from a four-and-a-half-foot dingus with rubber spikes to a copy of *Naughty Marie, the Upstairs Maid*. In the peep show you could watch people who did strange and wondrous things to themselves and to the occasional hoofed mammal.

Boris headed straight to the counter and handed the ugly attendant a five-dollar bill and got a stack of quarters to play with. He zipped into one of the booths, but didn't stay more than a minute.

The strolling change guy was walking around, banging on stalls.

"Ya can't window-shop here," he yelled. "Let's use 'em up!"

Boris came out of the booth next to the shouter and banged the door into his arm.

"Watch yourself there, meatball," the shouter said.

Boris looked embarrassed and headed for the back of the place, where the crowd thinned out and people didn't shout at you when you came out of your closet. I watched him go into another booth.

I went over to it and stood next to the door. There was no one else around, so I knocked on the door and said, "Hey, meatball, get outta there."

Boris opened the door.

"Did you bring the popcorn?" I said and stepped into the booth. Boris looked stunned. Next to him on the floor was the leather case. I reached down and grabbed it, smiling all the while.

"Well, move over," I said. On the screen, a large male

mutant was attacking a pair of female mutants with gusto. They must have used him as the model for the four-foot dingus. Boris reached for the leather case.

I raised a finger. "Let's not be selfish, Boris," I said and looked inside. There was an awful lot of American money in the case. On the screen, another male mutant entered the picture.

"The plot thickens," I said. Boris was looking around the booth as if he had suddenly remembered he had urgent business uptown. The picture clicked off and the booth went black.

"I know you won't yell," I said, fumbling for a quarter, "because if you yell, the owners will show up and then they'll call the cops and then the cops will show up and they'll want to know what a Russian diplomat was doing in a porn booth with me and this wad of money. And you'll make the morning edition of the *Post*, maybe even *Pravda*." I found a quarter and dropped it in the slot. The film started and the second male mutant began looking for his port in the storm. Boris held up both hands.

"Cigarette?" he asked.

"Go ahead."

He took a pack from his pocket and lit it with a lighter. "What did you sell to Kimberly Wyeth, Boris?"

"It is not Boris," he said, regaining a certain composure. He held up both hands again. "I do not understand what you are speaking to me. Here, identity. Okay?"

He reached slowly in his coat and pulled out a wallet. His name wasn't Boris. It was Gregor Strinsky and he wasn't a recent immigrant. Boris was a genuine Russian diplomat and a member in good standing of the United Nations.

"What did she buy, Boris?"

"You cannot do this to me!" he said sharply.

"You're right, Boris, I can't." The picture disappeared again. "Put in another quarter," I said. "It's your turn." I heard him sigh, but he put in the quarter. "I don't want to shatter any illusions, Boris, but you don't have diplomatic immunity in a dirty-book store. Now, what did she buy?"

"I will file protest," he said.

I opened the leather case and pulled out some of the

money. "Big bucks, Boris, *mucho dinero*." On screen, the mutants were getting rather sweaty, approaching the denouement, so to speak. Boris looked positively heartbroken staring at the money.

"So," I said, "what did she buy?"

"Ikons," he said. He pulled a handkerchief out of his coat and wiped off his face. He ran a hand through his hair and straightened his tie. Life was beautiful once again.

"You want to know what I think, Boris?"

"Why do you call me by that? My name is Gregor."

"Fine, Boris. You know what I think? I think you're indulging yourself in a little free enterprise. The kind of stuff that gets you ten to twenty in the freezer or wherever they're putting running-dog parasites these days."

That made him nervous. "Why are you so interested?"

"We're not negotiating a treaty, Boris. We're trying to decide whether or not you're telling me the truth."

"You enjoy frightening innocent people?"

"Boris, why was Wyeth buying ikons from you?"

"Because I had them for sale," he said, clearly astonished by my stupidity. "Maybe with the money, I will buy a house on Long Island."

"Wonderful, a budding suburbanite. You'll have to dress better first, maybe some nice polyester. Where did you get the ikons?"

"From Moscow," he said and smiled for the first time. "You have heard of it?"

"Is it close to Siberia?" I said and he stopped smiling.

"I have a girl friend in Moscow," he said. "She send them to me by courier. I sell them. We split money. Fifty-fifty, right?"

"You get them all from Moscow?"

"Yes."

"Maybe you were running a little short this month?"

"Short?"

"Maybe you stole some."

"No," he said, "no stealing."

"Maybe you stole one from a church in New Jersey, one that would bring you a lot of money?" I waved the bills in his face.

"No," he said.

93

The film ran out again and Boris said something in Russian and put in another quarter. On screen, the finale had been in earnest. I was positively amazed. So was Boris.

"You sure you didn't steal anything, Boris?"

"No stealing," he said.

"You're lying."

"No," he said, getting indignant. "What if I am?"

"I'll write your mother and tell on you."

He considered the idea.

"I cannot talk about it," he said. "Very important." He pointed to the leather case. "My business—nothing. Ikon is important."

I held up the money again. "Does this look like nothing to you, Boris?" He shrugged. "Why don't I just take you down to the FBI?"

He smiled. "You are not FBI."

"How do you know that?"

"I read *Time* magazine," he said smugly.

"You're right, Boris, I'm not with the FBI. Why won't you talk about the ikon?"

"You don't understand?"

"Do I sound like I understand?"

"We do not have ikon."

"Meaning you?"

"Naturally," he said.

"Naturally," I said, "but you want it?"

"It is ours. It was taken from us and we want it back."

"Who took it?"

"I do not know. It was a long time ago."

"Then why do you want it back now?"

"It belongs to Russia. The Americans will try to make propaganda with it, to show we try to smash the church. This is not true."

"Oh, hell, Boris, everybody knows you've been busting up churches since day one."

"No," he said, "it is not true. We try to join them together."

"I think you want it so you can sell it," I said.

Boris got really mad. "I am a Russian patriot. I will try to return it to the motherland. The Americans say they will return it if we negotiate. We do not trust them."

"Which Americans, Boris?"

"I have not been told this," he said. He dropped his cigarette to the floor.

"Take a guess, Boris. Who's got the ikon?"

"I do not like to guess about such things."

"What were you doing with Kimberly Wyeth tonight?"

"Business," Boris said. "A little free enterprise."

"Does she know where it is?"

Boris looked confused. "She tells me she knows. Maybe she does. She buys ikons for herself, and if she knows, she remembers me. Scratching everyone else's back. You know this?"

"And Kharkovnakov?"

Boris said something in Russian. "I am sorry," he said, "but Kharkovnakov works for your CIA."

"He doesn't work for the CIA, Boris."

"He would destroy the church for his own gain. The same thing. He hates his country, his own people."

"You didn't exactly make his life a bundle of joy, as I recall."

"He was anti-Soviet propagandist," Boris said, putting his fingers to his lips. "So, we kiss him off."

"Are you saying he's got it?"

"Perhaps you have it? Maybe you work for the CIA?"

"You read that in *Time* magazine, too?"

"I like *Time*," he said, "Brooke Shields. J.R. Ewing. *People* magazine."

"Enough, Boris."

"I do not understand your interest. Are you religious?"

"I'm a writer."

"A writer? Spy novels? James Bond?"

"Your brains are dribbling out your ears, Boris."

He grabbed for his right ear.

"Oh, Jesus." I took his hand away from his ear. The film ran out again, so I shoved in another quarter. A new film came on the screen. Same plot, though.

"What do you know about Martin Angle?" I said.

"Angle? He has been our friend in the past. Now—" He made a shaky gesture with his hand. "We are not so sure. Perhaps he stole the ikon?"

"I wondered if that crossed your mind."

"He has a great fortune, Angle. Very strong—in Moscow, in Washington." He said something else in Russian. "He keeps things for himself. He plays with both of us for profit."

"You ever meet him?"

"Once, maybe twice. In Washington, D.C."

"Ever do business with him? Sell him an ikon or two?"

"I do not care for Mr. Martin Angle," he said. "But what could I say?" He pressed his mouth closed. "It would do no good to say such things too much."

"Would they chop you in tiny pieces and mail you home?"

"Cuba," Boris said and made a face. "Cutting sugar cane."

"Have you tried to get the ikon before?"

"From the priest?" Boris said, "Yes. He wanted to do it, I think, but there was too much pressure. Then—" Boris snapped his fingers.

"You mean Father Nicholas?"

"No, no," he said. "The one who died." He snapped his fingers again. "The new one—Nicholas—he is not so reasonable. He works for Kharkovnakov and his fanatics. You know them, yes?"

"We met," I said.

"Then you understand."

"Yes," I said. "You don't know who has the ikon?"

"No," he said, "Now, may I have my money back?"

"I'm going to hang onto it for a while, Boris."

"You are a thief," he said. "The perfect American."

"Nobody's perfect, Boris. If I gave you your money, you'd be one up on me. As it stands, I've got something you want. Maybe it'll come in handy one of these days. You never know. Insurance. You understand that word?"

"Insurance? Yes. Tell me, what is your name?"

"Hunter."

"I think you are a real son of a bitch, Hunter."

"I think you're one, too, Boris."

"Just like George Scott. One son of a bitch to another, right?"

"Sure, Boris," I said. "Why did Kimberly Wyeth have to slap your face in the parking lot?"

Boris had his answer ready. "Because she is a real son of a bitch, too," he said. He was almost happy about it.

I turned toward the door.

"We are finished?" Boris asked.

"For right now we are," I said. "See you around, Boris."

"Okay, Hunter," Boris said and dropped in another quarter.

I stepped out of the booth and bumped into the change guy again. He looked at me and shot a glance into the booth.

"The book was a lot better," I said before he could start in on me.

11

I FOUND A Chock Full o' Nuts where I could sit at the counter in a stupor and not be bothered. There were only two customers in the place, and I was one of them. The other one was sitting a couple of stools down, drinking coffee and thumbing through a copy of the *New York Post*. He looked like an off-duty cop, a little thick around the middle, heavy face, dressed in a plain black suit. Every few minutes, he would scratch his cheeks, leaving pink tracks across his sallow skin.

I got a cup of tea and forgot about him. The radio in the kitchen played something loud and latin. The cigarette machine was out of order. The waitress was in the kitchen, laughing with the cook through the order window.

The *Post* landed on the counter next to my elbow. I glanced at the headline: "Mad Dog Butcher Nabbed." Catchy.

"You like current events?" the guy in the black suit asked.

"Is this a news quiz?"

"Nah," he said and slid onto the stool next to mine. "I'm working my way through college selling subscriptions."

"I'm not very interested," I said, "but thanks for asking."

"I can see that," he said and went right on sitting there. You just never know in New York. "What *are* you interested in, Hunter?"

"Gabe Pressman, right?"

He ignored my comment and jabbed a thick forefinger at the front page. Mad Dog looked like someone who shot rats for a living and did very well at it.

"This is a real monster," he said. "He shot fourteen, maybe fifteen people. Me? Seven tops. Nothing like this guy. He blows them away on their front porch. Guy'll be sitting down with a can of beer, watching the sunset. Next thing you know, he's got five, six holes in him."

"I just know there's a message in there for me."

"Nah," he said, "I'm just talking. That Mercedes yours?"

"No," I said, shaking my head. The waitress and the cook took momentary interest in us as a couple through the order window, then continued their conversation out of sight.

"Always wanted to drive one of them," he said. "How's it ride?"

"Smooth."

"I'll bet it does," he said and reached in his pocket. I sat up abruptly. "You nervous, Hunter?"

He took out a small photograph and laid it on the counter. It was Kimberly Wyeth.

"Oh, look," I said, "a Cybill Shepherd clone."

He put another picture on top of Kimberly. It was Boris in a tux.

"He looks like he owes somebody money," I said, innocently.

"How about this one?"

It was Martin Angle. "Nope."

"You sure?"

"Are you casting for a movie?"

He put his pictures away. "What's that you're drinking?"

"Tea with milk. It calms my nerves."

"Looks like shit," he said.

"You know, if you give me a day or two, I just know I could figure out what your position is on the planet."

"I'm one of the good guys," he said. "That's how come I get to stand around in the slush while you ride all over town in a Mercedes dressed like a fucking cowboy."

"I get it," I said. "You're here to intimidate me."

He smiled. "How I'm doing?"

"Not so good."

"I told them I didn't think it would work. This other guy wanted to whack you right out."

"There's more than one of you?"

"Are you kidding? There's a goddam department. But this other guy, he's got an eight-foot hard-on about you. I think he belongs in a bird cage myself."

"I'd love a job like yours," I said. "Sit around, read the paper, do bad-guy imitations. Must be a great life."

"Sure," he said, "This is a new technique I'm trying out. I figure if somebody like you will listen to reason, maybe it'll open up a whole new line for me. So, why not? If this was banana land, I'd have shot you, no problem. Here, people'd get upset if a guy got gunned down in a Chock Full o' Nuts."

"Do I beg for mercy now? I don't want to rush you or anything."

"Personally, I don't give a shit what you do. But this guy, the one with the hard-on, he wants you to avoid the new friends you don't know. He'd like you to go back to Jersey and diddle your cows or whatever the hell you do in Jersey."

"Did he say why?"

"National security."

"That's a little vague."

"Yeah, I know."

"You're with the government," I said, trying to sound shocked.

"Did I say that?"

"Not in so many words."

"And I thought I was being very obtuse."

"CIA?"

He made a see-saw gesture with his hand. "National security," he said.

"Last time I heard that word, we bombed Cambodia."

"Blew those little yellow fuckers all to hell," he said with a grin. "So, we get straightened out?"

"That's one way of looking at it."

"There's another way?"

"I could tell you to shove it straight up your ass."

He laughed. "I bet you could. But I'd have to go back and listen to this asshole tell me what a lousy job I've been doing. Maybe miss a promotion or two."

"You could lie."

100

"This other guy'd still want your dick on a platter. . . .
You going to read the paper?"

"Probably not."

"I'll take it with me," he said, getting off the stool. He
grabbed his coat and looked through the window at the
snow. "I should move to fucking Arizona."

"Should I hire a bodyguard or something?"

"I wouldn't get carried away. You could stop putting
your business in the street, you know what I mean?"

"You mean stay away from Martin Angle?"

"What do I know, I'm just part of the entertainment."
He put on his coat. "But you're lucky, I got to give you
that. If this was some crummy place like Athens, I'd've put
three slugs in the back of your head before you took your
first sip of that shit."

"Must be my lucky day."

"Don't count on it lasting too long," he said.

As I walked back to the hotel, dodging shadows and a
growing sense of paranoia, I tried putting things in their
logical holes. On the surface, it looked as if about half a
million people wanted the ikon. Nearly as many could
have stolen it in the first place. The only ones I was certain
weren't involved at all were the Chinese and the Knights
of Columbus.

There was the thug in the coffee shop who didn't fit into
any category I knew of; Martin Angle, who was no day at
the beach; Mary Sunshine aka Kimberly Wyeth, who probably wouldn't improve with age; Boris, the flaky Russian;
Kharkovnakov, Chernetzsky, Nicholas—and for all I
knew, the Philadelphia Fife and Drum Corps.

I dragged myself up to my room. It was exactly the same
as I left it—small, white and inexplicably dingy. I called
Jamie but she wasn't home. I called Haddonford, let it ring
once and hung up. I realized I didn't want to talk to anybody.

The early news came on and was right up to scratch covering the latest shenanigans in the Big Apple. A pair of
teenage gangsters had shot up a West Side grocery store,
wounding the owner and mutilating six cases of fresh fruit
in the process; the reporter did his stand-up in front of a

101

case of bleeding cantaloupes. A Brooklyn girl was arrested running naked through the lobby of the Citicorp building on her lunch hour, high on a controlled substance; she'd just broken up with her boyfriend and this was her way of making a statement about the situation, she said.

I had a clear decision to make. I could flush my head in the toilet several times or I could go to bed. The toilet looked inviting but I went to bed.

I didn't sleep very well, because about two hours later someone turned on the lights in my room. I had the words "What the hell is going on?" in my mouth when someone hit me very hard on the side of the head with a blunt object and the words blew up in my face. When my head stopped ringing and I had begun to uncoil from my fetal crouch, I saw the world through a red mist.

Boris sat at the foot of the bed holding a small blackjack in his hand. Boris looked a little dismayed. He probably hated violence as much as I did.

"Did you think I would let you run away with my money?" he said.

"I thought you'd be a sport about it."

"Not about money," he said.

"Could you put that thing back in your pocket? It's making me nervous."

"That is what it should do," Boris said, putting it away. "I am sorry I had to hit you. I wanted to get your attention." He took a flask out of his other pocket. "Would you like a drink?"

"Is it poisoned?"

He smiled and took a long sip before handing it to me. I took a drink and shivered. It tasted like grain alcohol.

"Russian vodka," he said. "Very good for you. Calms the nerves."

"I think I understand you, Boris."

"Yes, I agree."

"Your English got better, too."

"Americans think we speak like cartoons. Most of us do very well, I think."

"Who are you exactly, Boris?"

"I organize parties and exhibitions at the United Nations to show how sophisticated and modern we are. Those

102

of us who live in a socialist paradise have to keep up appearances. I really am a valuable asset to the state."

"Don't overdo the cynicism, Boris."

"You still call me Boris, even when you know my name. I should feel insulted but I don't. I like you."

"I'm glad."

"Where is my money?"

"In the first drawer of the dresser. Under the Bible."

Boris got his money.

"Do you mind if I try walking?" I said. "Since we've become such close friends and everything."

"Of course. Do you need some help?"

"I think I can manage." I rolled off the bed and immediately rolled back on it. "Maybe I'd better wait a minute. Where's your girl friend?"

"Kimberly?" he said and shrugged. "How should I know?"

"Doesn't she work for you?"

"On occasion she has been very helpful, but, no, she does not work for me. She is very independent."

"She runs errands for Martin Angle, too."

"You have not told me anything I do not know. Who do you work for, Hunter?"

"I'm a free spirit, just like Kimberly."

"I find that very difficult to believe," he said.

Boris looked as if he was ready to coax a different answer out of me. I got ready to jump if he tried.

"We have a serious problem here," he said.

"We don't have a problem at all, Boris. I don't work for anybody but me. We can fight over it, but it won't change my answer."

"If you do not work for anyone, Hunter, then why are you looking for our ikon with such determination?"

"I was trying to write a story," I said. "The next thing I knew, half a dozen Russian thugs tried to beat me up. Martin Angle wanted to shoot me with an empty gun. You want to be my buddy, and Kimberly's probably got one or two ideas herself. I don't know, Boris, maybe I'm just not used to all this attention."

"Do you always take things so personally, Hunter?"

"Should I just call it a day and go home?"

"I would not give up so easily," he said. "We might be able to help one another. We are after the same thing."

"I'm not interested in taking over the world."

"Neither am I, Hunter. I have an interest in all this. It is also part of my job. The better I do it, the more privilege I receive. No ideology. We all live in an imperfect world. We must try to make the best of it."

"And if we can make a little money on the side, then it's damn near peachy keen."

"See?" he said. "We think alike."

"No, we don't, Boris, but I'm listening."

"I think Martin Angle has the ikon."

"That would be my guess, but there are a few other people who might have it as well."

"We must start someplace," he said. "See, we do think alike. Kimberly has worked for Angle. I know this. But she has no loyalty and she would be quite capable of taking it."

"She's not all there," I said, tapping the undamaged portion of my skull.

"Perhaps," he said. "I do not think about her that much. Who else would like the ikon?"

"Kharkovnakov."

"So many," he said. "Tell me, Hunter, would it be worth twenty-five thousand dollars for you to find it first?"

"Why not save your money and do it yourself? It's your business."

"It would not be that easy for me."

"You seem to be doing just fine as far as I can tell."

"Please, Hunter. I have made you a substantial offer."

"But you haven't said why it's so important."

"I told you the truth. It is a symbol. Kharkovnakov will try to use it to embarrass us in any way he can. If he succeeds, a great many people will be hurt, both here and in Russia."

"I can't see Nicholas letting him do that."

"The priest? You are not thinking correctly. He cannot do anything. He tempers their plans, perhaps he even convinces them to hold back, but in the end he has no power except what Kharkovnakov gives him. We know all about him. He is playing a very dangerous game with Kharkovnakov, but he is harmless."

104

"What are you going to do if you get the ikon, Boris?"

"Return it to the motherland, of course," he said.

"That's the worst lie you've told me so far."

Boris laughed. "You have a good attitude, Hunter. I do not quite know what I will do with it. That is the truth. It would depend very much on what I am offered." He tossed the leather case on the bed. "There is fifteen thousand dollars. A down payment."

"I'll think about it."

"There could be more, Hunter."

"You're starting to sound like Martin Angle." I tossed the case back to him. "I said I'd think about it."

He looked at me shrewdly. "Do not think too much," he said. "Now, I must go. I hope tomorrow will be a better day for us all."

He stopped in front of the mirror and straightened out his hair.

"Tell me, Boris," I said when he opened the door, "are you with the KGB?"

"Of course," he said. "Aren't we all?"

He closed the door behind him and opened it two seconds later.

"Put a chair against your door tonight, Hunter," he said. "The security in this hotel is very bad."

It was nearly four in the morning before I settled into bed again. A few things were becoming clearer:

People were willing to kill to get the ikon, and I stood a very good chance of becoming one of the deceased.

Whether it was authentic or not seemed to make little difference.

Boris was a liar.

But so was Arnold Haddonford.

Life was turning out to be just full of surprises.

12

I RETURNED the car to Arnold Haddonford late the next morning. Conrad accepted the keys from me, not bothering to hide his surprise that I had returned them at all.

Haddonford was in the living room, drinking his morning glass of wine. He smiled and looked concerned.

"Would you like some wine, Hunter?" he said, "It appears you've had a long night." He reached for the bottle.

"No wine, Arnold," I said. His hand curled away from the bottle.

"Is something wrong?"

I went to the window. Below me, a taxi ran a red light and nearly hit a small group of pedestrians. The pedestrians shook their fists in anger. The taxi kept right on going.

"You lied to me, Arnold," I said without turning around. "Kimberly Wyeth isn't confused. She's a thief." Slowly, like a man delivering a bad business report, I told him what had happened.

When I turned around at last, Arnold Haddonford was staring down silently at his hands, clutched together on his lap to keep them from trembling too much. He raised his head and looked at me with sad empty eyes.

"I'm a foolish old man," he said. "I apologize, Hunter. I don't know what I thought I was doing."

"You're not a fool, Arnold."

"I *knew* she was involved with Angle. I don't know why I didn't tell you everything before. I thought perhaps you might prove me wrong." He put his hands on the arms of the chair. "I've never felt like such a complete idiot in my entire life."

"Are you still in love with her?"

"Yes," he said, with only a hint of a smile, "I suppose I am."

"It was almost a year ago," he continued, "when I was in England. I stay there once a year, usually in the spring. I don't know why I still do it. The people seem so sad these days, as if they know everything has become a parody of what it once was. They go through the motions of being British, and every day the country slides further into decline. It's a terrifying thing to see."

He stopped to wipe his face with a handkerchief.

"Last year, I had an unexpected visitor," he said, "from Interpol. He came to talk to me about Kimberly Wyeth. I thought it was a bit odd, but I was curious. I hadn't seen her in some time. I would call her up every several months, in Washington, hoping I might persuade her to visit me in New York. She never did, of course, but I accepted that. She was busy traveling, buying trips. I'd grown used to it."

"What did Interpol want with her?"

"The man asked me when I'd seen her last, if I knew any of her friends, if I'd heard anything about her recently. The usual sort of questions policemen ask all over the world."

He reached for the bottle of wine. "This is very difficult for me," he said.

I stopped his hand. "Not now, Arnold. Tell me what he said."

Arnold grabbed the bottle of wine and stared at me in defiance. "Dammit," he said, "I want a glass of wine." He filled his glass, drank it and continued.

"As I was saying, it was really quite fantastic. He told me that Interpol suspected her of stealing artwork— among other things. There had been a series of thefts, he said, jewels, money, paintings, some minor, one or two major ones. Do you remember the Picasso sculptures that were stolen in Paris last year?"

"Vaguely."

"It seems that Kimberly's travels corresponded precisely with each of the thefts. In each particular case, she knew the victims, some of them quite well. Very circumstantial, he said, but enough to interest Interpol. There was more. There always is these days."

He poured himself a little more wine. I didn't try to stop him.

"He told me that some of the stolen money had found its way to the Red Brigades, in Rome. Again, there was nothing concrete, no proof, no witnesses. And Interpol can't go after the stepdaughter of an American Secretary of State— even a dead one—without proof. The repercussions would be enormous. Do you know anything about the Brigades, Hunter?"

"I know who they are," I said.

"They're usually a crude bunch—and rather stupid, despite a success or two. Shooting the kneecaps off local judges is more their style. Anyway, there was a political killing that Interpol was very much interested in. The victim was the son of an Italian banker. The banker was very vocal in his opposition to the Brigades. I believe his bank even posted a substantial reward for information on them. They asked me about it."

"Kimberly knew the son," I said.

"Yes. She was seen with him several days before he died. His father found him, in his apartment. By the time the body was discovered, Kimberly had left the country."

"What did you tell Interpol?"

"I had nothing to tell them," he said. "I refused to believe she was involved. I knew about her radical friends, but given the state of things over there, I could name you a dozen young women like Kimberly who have behaved just as badly."

"Most of them haven't led anybody to the slaughter lately," I said.

"Yes," he said quietly. "In any case, I blocked the whole thing from my mind. When you told me that you'd seen her with Angle, I thought—I don't know what I thought—that she was being used, manipulated, that it was all a mistake. But after this morning, I see I was wrong. Terribly wrong."

"This morning?"

Arnold smiled sadly. "She was here."

108

"How'd it go?"

"She asked about you, Hunter, wanted to know who you were. I told her I didn't know anything."

"I'm becoming a real popular fellow these days. I should try for the Donahue show."

"She said she missed me," Arnold said and punched a button on his chair. Conrad came into the living room wearing an apron, his hands covered with flour. Arnold pointed to the wine.

"Please take this away, Conrad," he said. "And bring me a cup of coffee. No, bring me a pot."

Conrad picked up the wine and stared at me as if I'd done something unforgivable. I wondered if I had.

When we were alone again, Arnold asked, "What will you do now, Hunter?"

"Go home, get some rest."

"Are you going to continue with this?"

"Yes."

"I thought you would," he said. "I've put you in some danger, I know. My behavior has been inexcusable. I hope you can forgive me." He smiled again, the same sad smile. "I slept with her, you know. In Zurich, that first time."

"Forget about it, Arnold."

He stopped smiling.

"Perhaps you can tell me how to do that," he said.

I had some time to kill before the train, so I decided to buy Jamie a present. I went to Saks. With fifty dollars and my Lucky Seven Decoder Ring I could probably buy her a belt buckle. I wandered around the main floor until I came to the scarf department. A middle-aged woman with a healthy disrespect for my appearance told me to take my time. The next time I walk into Saks, I'm going to bring a crate of chickens and see if I can make an even trade. I thumbed through the merchandise and finally found one for thirty-five dollars. I held it up and saw Kimberly Wyeth staring at me from the end of the counter. She looked distraught.

"Do you like this one?" I asked.

She came over. "For yourself?" she said.

"No."

She felt it. "It isn't silk."

"Neither is a sow's ear," I said.

Up close, she looked a little less distraught and a little more stunning. She was dressed in a full-length fox coat with her hair pulled back to one side by a simple gold mesh band that couldn't have cost more than a grand.

"I need your help," she said and put her hand on my arm.

"I left my white horse at home."

Her fingers tightened around my arm. "Martin Angle is going to kill me," she said, her voice getting louder.

"You work for him, Kimberly," I said. "He's not going to kill you for that."

"He thinks I know where the ikon is. He said he'd kill me if I didn't tell him."

"So tell him."

"I don't know," she said and a single tear rolled down her cheek. Oh my, I thought, and forgot about the scarf.

I dragged her out of Saks and headed for the skating rink at Rockefeller Plaza. Once we got inside she stopped crying. By the time we got to the rink, she was positively frisky.

"I heard you saw Arnold today."

"He's such a dear man," she said, "and I was curious about you."

"Find out anything interesting?"

"Absolutely," she said, taking out a joint. "Like some?"

"Not right at the moment."

She lit it and took a long drag. "Will you protect me, Hunter? I have to know that."

"Depends on your story," I said.

"I've already told you," she said and took another drag. "Angle wants to kill me. Isn't that enough?"

"Tell me again why he wants to kill you."

"He thinks I know where the ikon is. How would I know where it is?"

"Because you buy and sell them. You picked up a load the other night on the West Side."

Her mouth dropped a little. "That motherfucker," she said.

"I liked you better when you were scared to death."

"Did Gregor tell you that?"

"More or less. I also know about your Roman holiday. The damsel-in-distress act is wearing a little thin. It was pretty good, though. The tear was a nice touch."

She sucked furiously on the joint. "You're not half as cute as you think, Hunter."

"Somebody in a Chock Full o' Nuts said the same thing."

"Did they bother to tell you who's got the ikon?"

"This sounds like a fun game. Are you going to tell me?"

"The priest," she said.

"Nicholas?"

"I know he told you it was stolen."

"That's not what he said."

"Then he lied. He was going to sell it to Martin but changed his mind."

"And now everybody's coming after you."

"Yes," she said, "and I don't like it."

"Who do you want me to shoot first? Angle? The Russian?"

"Both," she said. "I'll pay you fifty thousand dollars to do it. Cash."

"My price keeps going up," I said. "Boris offered me half that to find the ikon for him."

"Who the hell is Boris?"

"Gregor. I call him that because we're buddies."

"I'm in a position to offer you more," she said. "I know people who would be willing to pay a lot of money for the ikon."

"What about your tender white body? Do I get that, too?"

"I live a few blocks from here," she said. "I could let you have a preview." She ran her tongue lightly over her lips.

"I'll pass," I said. "I'd probably end up like that poor bastard in Rome."

Kimberly tried to slap me, but I grabbed her hand and brought it slowly down to the railing.

"Cocksucker," she said.

"Kimberly, what would your father have said if he heard you?"

"Absolutely nothing," she said. "Daddy was a cocksucker just like you."

13

KIMBERLY VANISHED into the crowd, but her scent stayed with me, a strange mixture of high-priced dope and perfume. The skaters swirled around the ice in time to the music. I watched an attractive young couple gliding backward along the edge and contemplated man's relationship with the universe and why God made little green apples like Kimberly Wyeth. I reached no conclusions except that I needed a long nap and the sorts of things that only money could buy. I started making a list and stopped at a sixty-five-foot gaff-rigged motor sailer.

I dragged myself to Fifth and stole a cab from two South American gentlemen who appeared to be high on something a little more potent than life itself. At Penn Station I waited around with the rest of the herd until they called my train. I got on it and promptly fell asleep until the conductor woke me up outside New Brunswick to tell me that the next stop was mine.

I went directly home, put some food in Jules' bowl and crawled upstairs into my bed. Over the years, I've discovered that sleep is the perfect response to the stress of these hectic modern times. If people followed my example, three-quarters of the world would have been continually out of it since before 1940.

I'd been dozing for a few hours when the phone rang.

"Hunter," Jamie's secretary said, "you're home?"

"This is a recording," I said.

"You'd better get over here."

"What is it now?"

"I'm not sure," she said, "but there are two guys in Brooks Brothers suits in her office and they want to talk to you."

"Were they polite?"

"No," she said. "I think they're with the government."

The one who did the talking was named Ed Conshocken. He didn't introduce his partner, referring to him only as "Let me see that file," or "Did you get that?" His partner didn't speak. Maybe he had a voice like Daffy Duck.

Jamie looked annoyed. She sat behind her desk and, when the two bozos weren't looking, slid her finger across her throat and pointed it at me. I interpreted her body language to mean she was upset.

Conshocken didn't waste any time.

"We'd like to know what your interest is in Gregor Strinsky."

I looked at Jamie. "Do I have to tell him anything?"

"You'd damn well better," she said.

"I want to see some identification."

"Hunter," Jamie said, "they're from the government. I've seen their ID."

"The government's a big place," I said. "They could be with the Forest Rangers." I pointed at the duck. "Maybe that one's Smokey the Bear."

"Why don't you just answer the question," Conshocken said. He was middle-aged and stocky and acted as if he was accustomed to dealing with lesser beings. He asked questions as if he expected the answers to come back to him wrapped in plastic.

"Why don't I go back home to my nap."

"Let me have it," Conshocken said to the duck. The duck produced two sets of credentials from an enormous briefcase on the floor and passed them over to me. They said they were from the State Department.

"Since when does State get to question civilians about Soviet agents before the FBI takes a crack at them?"

"Would you like the FBI to question you, Hunter?" Conshocken said. "Are you aware of the penalties for associating with known Soviet operatives?"

"At least with the FBI I'd know what kind of insults to use. What do you do over there in Foggy Bottom?"

"I can't answer that," Conshocken said.

I grinned.

114

"I know you," I said. "You're the guy with the eight-foot hard-on." I turned to Jamie. "He's a spook. I could be wrong, of course. He could just be another jerk in a blue suit. The thug in Chock Full o' Nuts wasn't that specific."

"Hunter," Jamie said. She was telling me to be careful.

"A spook," I said. "A spy." I noticed Conshocken's partner squirming in his chair. "Blow your cover?" He stopped squirming. "I thought you guys just sat around cutting clips from *Soviet Life* and writing dumb comments in the margins."

Ed Conshocken coughed, a rather polite cough under the circumstances.

He kept his eyes on me and stuck out his hand in the general direction of the turkey. "Could I have that file on Hunter," he said. He opened the file, skimmed several pages and began to read.

"On March 27, 1971, you gave a speech before Sigma Delta Chi at the University of Missouri in which you described Henry Kissinger as a 'habitual war criminal.' In addition, you suggested that if everyone in the audience would make up voodoo dolls of Dr. Kissinger and stick pins in them—I'm quoting here—'we could save the Swedes a lot of money and the world a lot of misery.' End quote.

"You've known several, if not all, of the Weather Underground. In 1972, you conducted a series of clandestine interviews with the group; they were published in a well-known leftist music publication. There's more, of course, but we'll move ahead.

"You haven't been active in any antigovernment activities since moving to Raven Rock, New Jersey, in 1975, until you were observed in the company of a known Soviet agent operating out of the United Nations named Gregor Strinsky. Earlier, you accused a well-known American businessman, a Mr. Martin Angle, of being a Russian spy and of stealing several pieces of art. You physically abused one of his employees." Conshocken closed the file dramatically. "We'd like to know what you're trying to do."

"Watch my lips," I said. "What I do is none of your business. Did you get all that?"

The duck nodded, scribbling furiously in a notebook.

"I think I'd like a word with Mr. Hunter," Jamie said. "If that's all right with you gentlemen?"

A trace of amusement appeared on Conshocken's face.

"I'd read him the whole book if I were you, Miss Hale," he said.

I followed Jamie into Hangly's office. He was at his desk.

"Hi," he said.

"Forget we're here," Jamie said. Hangly did nothing of the sort.

"Did you have a lobotomy while you were in New York or what?" she said.

"I don't like them."

"That isn't relevant, Hunter. People who hang around with Russian spies end up in jail."

Hangly's mouth opened and closed quickly. He looked like a frog going after a fly.

"Nobody's going to jail," I said.

"That's a relief," she said, sidestepping to Hangly's desk. "They're going to start a file on *me*, Hunter."

"They're trying to scare you, Jamie."

"They're doing a damn good job," she said, looking at Hangly. He pretended to go back to work. "What were you doing with a Russian spy, for Christ's sake? I thought you were looking for a stolen ikon."

"It's gotten a little complicated."

"That's the first intelligent thing you've said so far."

I told her approximately what had happened in New York. Hangly's jaw began its slow descent toward his desk top while I described my meeting with Angle, Boris and the porn booth, Kimberly and the rest of the fun I'd been having for the past twenty-four hours.

"I can see why they're interested in you," Jamie said.

"Beyond stuffing me in a mason jar? I wouldn't begin to know."

"Why don't you ask them?" Hangly said.

"Ask them what?"

"Ask them what they want. It seems they're stalling for something. At least that's how it appears to me."

"What else, Hangly?" I said. I should know better than to give encouragement to a Harvard grad. They think it's an excuse to submit a grant proposal.

"I think if there was any real possibility here of Hunter's doing business with the Russians," Hangly said, "two scenarios would occur. One, nothing would happen. They'd wait until they caught you with the goods or whatever. Or two, the FBI would have you in a room somewhere, asking pointed questions. They'd grill you like a scrambled egg and offer you a deal. At least that's how I see it."

Jamie and I were stunned into silence.

"Something wrong with my input?" Hangly asked.

"Oh, no," I said, "your input was fine. Grill me like a scrambled egg?"

"I frequently get carried away with my scenarios."

"Why don't we turn Hangly loose on those two clowns?" I said to no one in particular.

"What would you do in *this* scenario?" Jamie asked.

"Give me a little more information on those guys in there," Hangly said. We did, and he thought about it carefully.

"Simple," he said and explained his scenario. We thrashed it around for a minute and came up with a better one.

A real gem.

For openers, we pulled an Ehrlichman-Haldeman. She played bad cop and I played good cop. I started out with an apology which made Conshocken positively glow.

"That may be fine from your point of view," Jamie said to him, "but I'm not entirely convinced you have any legal standing here."

"I'm not sure I understand what you're driving at," Conshocken said cautiously.

"I think you're on a fishing trip. Hunter is a legitimate journalist working on a legitimate story and you're trying to intimidate him." She waited two beats and added, "I think I'd like the name of your superior. If that isn't too much trouble."

"Hey, come on, Jamie," I said. "All they want is a little information."

"Are you prepared to hand over your notes to them?" she asked sharply.

"No. But they don't want my notes, right?"

The duck handled that one. He nodded his head no.

117

Maybe I could trade him for a scarf at Saks, I thought. He'd make somebody a nice pet.

Conshocken looked at us coolly. "Why this sudden change?"

"No change," I said. "I decided it wasn't worth the effort. I don't know anything, so I can't tell you anything. She's the one playing hardball. Ask her."

Jamie folded her hands together and did a perfect imitation of a lawyer. "I spoke to an old friend of mine about the situation. He explained a few things." She looked at her watch. "I think he should be here soon. Would anyone like some coffee while we wait?"

"Who did you talk to about this?" Conshocken asked.

"Cream and sugar?" Jamie said to him.

Twenty minutes later, a man who looked big enough to be a professional wrestler walked through the door of Jamie's office. He had closely cut salt-and-pepper hair and acted like a field commander surveying the troops after a losing battle. He looked over the room and seized upon the duck.

"My name is Reynolds," he said. "I'm from the Bureau." Conshocken's face went a little white and the duck started to twitch. "Now, what's all this happy horseshit about some goddam Russian spy?"

Conshocken glared at Jamie. "This wasn't necessary," he said.

"Who are you?" Reynolds asked. Conshocken started to answer but gave up. He stuck out his hand and the duck laid the credentials on his palm one more time.

"State Department," Reynolds said with a chuckle. "You boys are way out of your jurisdiction. Congress says so."

"We're looking for information," Conshocken said.

"Aren't we all?" Reynolds observed. He took out a cigar and lit it.

"Let me see some identification," Conshocken said, a little spitefully I thought.

Reynolds handed Conshocken a small leather wallet. He took it, examined it and gave it back.

"Now," Reynolds said, "You want to tell me what you're doing?"

118

"We think Hunter is about to disrupt an investigation of Soviet activity that may involve some former State Department personnel. We'd like him to stop. Naturally, our involvement is only semiofficial."

"You Hunter?" Reynolds said to me.

"Yes."

"Didn't you write some books?"

"I did."

"What were you doing with the Russian?"

"The Russian happened to pop up. It was a big surprise to me, too."

"What kind of story are you working on?"

"Somebody stole an ikon. I'm trying to find out who."

"How exactly did this Russian 'pop up?' "

"Through a woman named Kimberly Wyeth—she's the stepdaughter of James Enderson the late Secretary of State—and Martin Angle. He's an art collector, and he used to work with Kimberly's dad. He's a prick."

"Interesting line of work," Reynolds said. "Angle's with the Russians?"

"Of course not," Conshocken muttered.

"I don't know who Angle's with," I said. "He's capable of anything."

"This is completely absurd," Conshocken said.

"What's his connection with this ikon you're looking for?" Reynolds asked, ignoring him.

"I think he stole it. Or had it stolen. Or knows where it is. Pick anyone you like. Kimberly Wyeth knows about it, too."

"Are you out of your mind?" Conshocken said.

Reynolds frowned. "I want to hear a little more about this 'semiofficial' investigation of yours."

"I can't tell you any more," Conshocken said. "It involves national security."

Reynolds surveyed our happy group. "You people got a real dog and pony show going here." He took a long drag on the cigar and blew a perfect smoke ring in the air. "I think I'd better talk to Washington on this one."

Conshocken's arm shot out. "File," he said and the duck scrambled for the briefcase, pawing through it frantically. Conshocken said, "Excuse me," and took it away from

119

him. He took out several sheets of paper and handed them to Reynolds. "I'd read this first," he said.

Reynolds skimmed the papers, nodding his head every now and again in total amazement.

"You've had Strinsky under surveillance for a year and you haven't done anything?"

"You weren't supposed to read it out loud," Conshocken said. He held out his hand for the papers, but Reynolds kept on reading.

"The stuff that passes for intelligence these days," Reynolds said. "You believe any of this crap?"

"I can see that this conversation is no longer productive," Conshocken said. The duck gathered all the papers together and stuffed them hurriedly in the briefcase.

"I'd like those back," Conshocken said to Reynolds. Reynolds folded them and put them in his coat pocket. "If you're from State, I'm with the Brownies," he said.

"I want those papers," Conshocken said loudly.

"You wouldn't want to take them from me, would you?" Reynolds asked.

Conshocken thought about it for a minute, gritted his teeth and walked out. Reynolds chuckled to himself, sat down and put his feet up on Jamie's desk.

"They told me when I retired from the Bureau that life wasn't going to be fun anymore," he said. "Now, Hunter, just what kind of horseshit have you got me involved in this time?"

After I told him, Reynolds said, "They look like spooks and they act like spooks but I'm not sure I know what they're doing. I'd bet even money that nobody else does either."

"You got that feeling, too," I said.

"Read this," Reynolds said and handed me the papers. All they said, in essence, was that Gregor Strinsky was a known KGB agent suspected of selling "religious artifacts" for his own private gain. They also mentioned Dimitri, the dud Russian spy, and suggested that Boris might have conspired with Dimitri to buy American technology.

"That's it?" I said.

"It isn't a report," Reynolds said, "it's a sideshow."

"Meant to scare us," Jamie said, taking the papers away from me.

"You're as smart as you are pretty," Reynolds said. "There are a couple more things that bothered me. The bit about him selling ikons or whatever he's selling. Here's this Russian, they got the goods on him and they haven't turned him in. Hell, they haven't even tried. Even the CIA doesn't let an opportunity like that pass by."

"Unless the CIA doesn't know about it," I said. "Unless Ed and Daffy want him all to themselves."

"Did you get smarter since I last saw you, Hunter, or am I just getting old?"

"Probably a little of both," I said.

"The other thing, Dimitri wasn't a spy any more than you are, Hunter."

"But they said he was a spy," Jamie said. "It was in all the papers."

"Nobody knows what he was, and the fact that he got his face on page one doesn't mean a whole lot. We needed the publicity. But Dimitri was strange. I don't think he even understood what he knew. He had lots of stories about money and meetings but nothing anybody could verify. Somebody was using him and using him good. We went over his story a hundred times and nothing showed. Not a crack. Nothing. Damnedest thing I ever worked on. That's why this Gregor intrigues me. You watch him, Hunter. If he's KGB, he's not a nice guy. He's playing a role for you."

"It's a pretty good act," I said.

"I haven't seen one that wasn't." He stood up. "I'm going back home. My bees are probably half frozen and I've got to make sure the smudge pots don't go out." He shook Jamie's hand. "See if you can't keep the boy in line. And you be careful, Hunter. Boris moves around a little too freely for my taste. You watch him."

"I will," I said and shook his hand. "Thanks."

"Bothered the hell out of those two, didn't we?"

"I'll call you if we need an encore."

"Nope," Reynolds said. "I'm getting too old for this foolishness."

Jamie had some work to finish up with Hangly, so I decided to go home, too. The duck fell in step with me as I turned the corner toward the parking lot.

"Ed wants a word with you," he said.

"You're talking," I said. "We all thought you sounded like Daffy Duck and that's why you didn't say anything."

"Ed doesn't like people talking when he's running things. He says it detracts from his aura of authority."

"How much are they paying you to bask in his aura, Daffy?"

"The name is Samuels," he said.

"That doesn't sound like nearly enough."

"You ought to keep your mouth shut, Hunter. Ed's a little upset with you right now."

I fished in my pocket and pulled out two nickels.

"What the hell is this?"

"Two nickels make a dime," I said. "Call somebody who cares."

Samuels just had to smile. "Where's the fed?"

"Went home," I said.

Conshocken was standing by my jeep, rubbing his hands together. He saw me and grinned. "Did you get the papers, Samuels?"

"No, sir," Samuels said. "Hunter here says the FBI guy went home."

"Give me the papers, Hunter," Conshocken said.

"You should say, 'May I see your papers, pleeze,' and the answer is no. Besides, I don't have them."

Conshocken slugged me, a low punch that doubled me up alongside the jeep. He grabbed my coat, reached inside and pulled out the papers. Then he yanked me up by the collar.

"I'm going to tell you something, asshole. Don't fuck with me anymore, you got that?"

"Bad day, huh, Ed?" I said and brought my knee up hard between his legs. Conshocken grunted and let go of me. While he was busy grabbing at his crotch, I turned to Samuels.

"You in this, Samuels?"

"You're crazy," he said and backed away. Conshocken was down on one knee, but trying to get up. I shoved him over with my foot.

Conshocken reached for something in his pocket. Samuels saw it before I did and grabbed his hand. The gun clattered on the pavement.

"Jesus Christ, Ed," Samuels said, picking it up.

"I'll kill him," Conshocken said. "I'll kill the son of a bitch."

I held my stomach, keeping the pain at bay. "Get him out of here before I run him over." I opened the door and climbed inside. Samuels pulled Conshocken to his feet and dragged him away. He started yelling and one or two people on the sidewalk stopped to listen. Samuels shoved him into one of the cars and took off.

I looked at myself in the rearview mirror. The face that stared back looked as if it needed a nap.

Jamie woke me up at seven-thirty that night. She and Jules were waiting patiently next to my bed. She kissed me on the cheek.

"What's for dinner?" she said.

Dinner turned out to be a ragged affair, thrown together from odds and ends left lurking in the refrigerator. After we ate, I stalked the house, unable to sit still. My stomach hurt a little, so I heated some water for tea and then turned off the water because I decided I really didn't want any tea. I pawed through the bookcase for something to read but the thought of all those words just made me nervous. I listened to the radio. I turned off the radio.

Jules and Jamie watched my antics.

"You're going to start bumping into things pretty soon," she said.

"Maybe I should go for a walk."

"Maybe you should give me a hug instead. I haven't had one all day."

I sat down next to her on the couch and put my arms around her.

"They have drugs for people in your condition," she said.

"I wish we had some. I want to be sedated."

Jules placed her head on Jamie's rear end.

"We have company," I said.

Jamie scratched Jules on her chin. The dog drooled in ecstasy. She *was* getting simple on me.

123

"Jules," I scolded.

"Now leave her alone," Jamie said.

"She misses you when you're not here," I said carefully, implications running amok. "I miss you, too."

"It took you long enough to say it," Jamie said, watching my reaction.

"I thought it was obvious."

"I know it's obvious, Hunter," she whispered, laughing a little. "I just like to hear it."

She started to say something else, changed her mind and moved closer.

"Do you really miss me, Hunter?"

"All the time."

"No, you don't. You're one of the most self-contained men I know. If I disappeared tomorrow, you'd miss me for a while but then you'd carry on with your life." She laid her head down. "You'd find somebody else," she said, answering her own questions, whatever they might be.

"Maybe," I said, "but I wouldn't want to."

She held me tight.

"Jamie?"

She sat up and kissed me. "Don't mind me," she said. "I'm just feeling vulnerable. I get to do that around here. That's part of the rules."

She pulled Jules off the couch and they padded across the floor to the stairs. I wanted to hold them both and never let go.

"I'm going to bed," Jamie said. "Come up soon, okay?"

The house was perfectly quiet. I opened the door to the stove, tossed in a few more logs and watched as the fire licked its way around the edges of the wood, listening to the snap of resin as it spit into the flames.

I glanced over at the kitchen window and saw something moving just beyond the glass, something that looked like a human face. In a second it was gone. That was enough.

I moved as quickly as I could, fear turning my legs to lead. Everything slowed down. My hand slipping on the knob, the door swinging by me in a blur, banging like thunder against the wall, stepping outside, terrified of turning my eyes, the cold air blasting into my face.

I looked, but saw only the soft pattern of light on the

124

hard snow. I went to get the flashlight. Outside again, I searched the ground beneath the window where the snow had turned to ice. Nothing. I couldn't stop. I followed the narrow path around the house to the river and swung the light across the ice.

I still didn't see anything, so I worked my way along the bank to the trees and back again. On the way to the house, I thought I heard something on the bridge. I ran, stumbling through the crusted snow until I reached the foot. The bridge was empty.

I walked across it, listening to the old wood creak in the bitter cold. At the other end, I stopped, a feeling of exhaustion settling over me.

Jamie was at the door with Jules beside her.

"What are you doing?"

"I thought I heard something."

She looked puzzled.

"Nothing," I said, "Just my imagination."

We got into bed and she curled around me. She was asleep in minutes. I felt the soft touch of her nightgown against my skin, the warm jet of her breath on my neck. I lay awake in the middle of the night, losing myself in her, feeling safe and protected. At least, that was what I kept telling myself.

In the morning, there was a fresh layer of snow on the ground, covering everything, hiding the traces of things that moved just below the surface.

14

I WOKE UP TO the smell of bacon and eggs and the sound of one of those subhuman rock bands blathering something excruciatingly mellow over the radio. I retreated to the relative safety of the bathroom and shut the door.

Of course, I was thinking about doing business with insane Russians carrying a five-hundred-year-old grudge, a vicious millionaire and a handful of government geeks. I jumped in the shower and ran the water until it got cold. The music was still on downstairs. Some things you have to get used to in this life.

Jamie filled my plate with scrambled eggs and bacon and sat down. She read the business section of the *Times* while I tackled the real news. I was in the middle of a fascinating article concerning the never-ending problems facing the Pacific Basin when she spoke.

"What are your plans for today?"

"I'm not sure yet."

"Feel like taking the day off?"

"I'm not sure I can, Jamie."

She turned the page menacingly.

"Why not?"

"I think I'm going back to Hermitage."

"I want to go with you."

"You can't."

"Why not?"

"That's the second time you've asked me that."

"And I haven't got an answer yet."

"You can't go because I'd worry too much with you there."

"So I can sit around and worry about you?"

"You'll be at work."

She was sadly amused. "Do you think that makes any

126

difference, that I'll get involved in some snazzy corporate deal and lose track of you?"

"Not this one, Jamie."

She threw the paper down. "Why, dammit?"

"Because I don't know what's going to happen!"

She looked at me angrily and left the table. A few minutes later, she stuck her head back in the greenhouse. She had her coat on.

"That's exactly why I want to go with you," she said.

I heard the door slam and watched her through the window as she walked down the riverbank. Jules was with her. Jamie kicked softly at the ice as she walked. Jules padded around, sniffing the new snow. I went to get my coat.

They hadn't gotten far.

"Feeling guilty?" she asked.

"Just lonesome."

We kicked the frozen ground together, looking for clues. We didn't find any. She shivered in the bright morning sun.

"Cold?"

"Freezing," she said.

I put my arms around her.

"Tell me you love me," she said quickly.

"I love you."

"Then be careful," she said. "Don't do anything stupid today."

She held onto her optimism until she was ready to leave for work. Standing there with her briefcase, she looked as if she'd lost her entire family.

"Everything will be all right," I said.

"A fat lot you know," she said and walked out the door, an orphan all grown up and leaving home.

I called her office later in the morning but she wasn't there.

"She said she was going to stay home and brood," her secretary said. "You two have another fight?"

"Nothing like that."

"Oh," she said, "then it's normal behavior."

"Tell her I'll call her later."

"That's a good idea."

Outside the sky was turning a clear blue, temperature moving up toward thirty degrees. A good day for a drive.

There were no mourners when I got to the church, no widows dressed in black, no thick-coated Russian families. On the hill the groundskeeper stood behind the old priest's grave holding a shovel in his hand and watching me, like some image from a forgotten photograph. I walked up the hill toward the grave.

He began shoveling snow away from the stone and continued working as if I weren't there, grunting with each shovelful. I swept off some snow from the small dome on top of the stone.

"I want to talk to Nicholas," I said. The shovel scraped along the ground. He tossed the snow aside and started on another pile. I grabbed the top of the handle.

"Not here," he said sullenly.

"Is he at Zemlya?"

"No," he said and walked away from the grave. I dropped the shovel and followed him as he hurried down the slope to the church. He climbed the front steps and took out his keys.

"I have to talk to him," I said. "Where is he?"

The groundskeeper pointed toward Hermitage. "Home," He said, opening the door and closing it quickly behind him. I could hear the lock fall.

I drove into Hermitage and parked in front of the store where I had gotten the cane. The woman remembered me and, crossing herself, told me where Nicholas lived. I took my time walking there. It was a small house, near the end of the street, stuck behind a row of birches.

I stepped up the walk to his door and rapped twice, the noise breaking out crisp and sharp in the cold air. When there was no answer, I tried the door. It opened and I went inside.

The shades were drawn and the house was dark. Except for the small ikon in the corner of the living room, the house might have belonged to my aunt, a nervous woman who grew as frightened of the daylight as she did of the night and eventually refused to move from her bedroom.

The furnishings were old and vaguely forlorn; the rooms suffocatingly warm.

I wandered, opening a drawer here and there, peering into closets, disturbing empty cabinets, the remnants of what seemed to be an uneventful life. A handful of magazines lay on the brown horsehair couch. A faded *Time* magazine lay open to an article on Russian dissidents.

A checkbook in one of the drawers caught my eye. Nicholas was poor. I put it back, embarrassed. The carpet, a blue-and-red floral design that no one had manufactured in years, was worn nearly through in the doorway leading to the kitchen.

The cupboards held a meager supply of food: soups, canned vegetables, a box of crackers. The refrigerator was empty except for a bottle of milk. There was a back door to a small yard and another door into the cellar. I opened it and a wave of frigid musty air blew up from below.

His bedroom was on the second floor, containing only a chest, a single bed and a nightstand. There was a Russian book on the stand, the binding snapped in two. In the closet, six shirts, four pairs of pants and a suit. I took a box down from the top shelf and discovered a black Russian fur hat made in Leningrad and copies of Kharkovnakov's books in the original Russian, autographed. The bindings were intact, the books unopened.

The door to the second room upstairs, next to the bathroom, was locked. I went downstairs to the kitchen and looked through the drawers and cupboards. On the wall of the stairs leading to the cellar, I found a handful of old keys on a piece of twine.

The fourth key slipped inside the old lock and the door creaked open.

An old kitchen chair sat in the middle of the bare room facing a mirror on the wall. There were minute scratches on the dusty wooden floor around the chair. A light bulb hung loosely from an outlet above. Unlike the rest of the house, the room was cold. I pressed my hand over the vent; it was shut off.

I imagined him coming into the room, turning on the light as he went. I did the same. I shut the door, walked to the chair, sat in it, faced the mirror and stared at my image four feet away. I kept watching myself. Despite the cold, I began to sweat. I shifted in the chair and stared at myself until I was no longer certain of who I was.

The room suddenly reminded me of an interrogation chamber, except that here the interrogator and the prisoner were the same person. What did someone like Nicholas do in a room like this?

I had thought of him as many things: naive, confused, a fool. All the time I had missed the essential truth; Nicholas was alone and I was sitting in his cloister.

I became aware of the rest of the house, its noises, the gentle whir of the furnace, the creaking of the joists in the heat, the feeling of sadness that permeated the sparse surroundings. I stared at the edges of the mirror and thought I saw something odd. I looked again. The mirror was pushed out from the wall at a strange angle.

I got up and lifted the mirror. Behind it, tucked into a slot in the back, was a small brown book. I pulled the mirror down and opened the book. Inside was a list of dates and figures stretching out over the last two years. The words were all in Russian and the same name seemed to appear over and over except for the last entry. The writing was different from the others and the figure next to it was substantially larger: $75,000. I stuck the book in my pocket and left.

I was downstairs, putting the keys back on their nail, when I heard footsteps coming up the walk and the sound of Russian voices; like me, robbers too late for the grave. I shut the door and crouched on the stairway. The voices rattled through the house, loud, unfamiliar. I moved farther down the stairs.

I heard them going through the living room, searching. Drawers banged open and shut, the sofa rumbled across the floor. One of them started walking into the kitchen. I moved into the dark cellar, stepping across the hard dirt floor toward the noise of the furnace. The Russian yanked the door open. I heard him say something and laugh. He stepped down the stairs, and a flashlight's beam whipped through the cellar. I sank down behind the furnace and waited.

Then, something fell, landing on the floor above me with

a heavy thud. Another voice called out, directly overhead. The Russian with the flashlight yelled back and kept walking slowly toward the furnace. The other Russian yelled again, more urgently. The flashlight beam swung away from me. I listened to his footsteps as he trudged back upstairs.

I moved quietly after him to the open door and peered around the edge. One of the Russians was holding something in his hand, waving it around. The other one caught his wrist and held his arm still. It was a small rectangular bundle wrapped in newspaper and tied with a string. The Russian took it away and opened the newspaper. He held up a handful of bills, spreading them open like a fan. The other Russian whispered something and touched the money.

Then they began arguing. The Russian with the money pushed the other one over to the couch. The one on the couch slammed his fist down on the cushion and then rubbed the side of his face with it. The one with the money pointed at the couch and yelled. The other one nodded reluctantly. Apparently he was going to stay.

The Russian with the money stuffed it in his coat and opened the front door. A few seconds later, he opened it and called his partner outside. They walked to the end of the sidewalk.

I rushed into the living room. The ikon in the corner lay broken on the floor. Like the mirror, the back of the ikon had been hollowed out. There were two compartments, one for the money and the other for something smaller.

I heard the Russian walking back up the sidewalk. I laid the ikon back on the floor and hurried into the kitchen and out the back door as quietly as I could. As I ran into the next yard, I realized what the other space was for.

A gun.

Zemlya was more lifeless than the cemetery. I banged on the locked gate and yelled at the house, but no one answered. The house seemed to have withdrawn, like some medieval castle getting ready for a siege. I was the last straggler, too late to be saved. I was almost back to the jeep when I heard the front door slam.

Kharkovnakov stepped across the yard with Misha beside him. The dog strained against a thick black leash.

He stopped a few feet from the fence and let the leash play out. The dog moved closer to me and crouched down in the snow, watching every move with quick jerks of his head. When I was five feet from the fence, the dog started to growl. The muscles on the back of his neck tensed and his heavy bottom jaw dropped open. I didn't come any closer.

Kharkovnakov didn't speak. There was no hatred in his eyes, no anger. I had become an abstraction to him, like the rest of the modern world. I wanted to come forward, to tell him that he had to stop whatever he was planning, that it was all hopeless. He must have found me a strange supplicant. I made no request, asked for nothing. If we spoke, I knew the words would be lost through the filter of centuries.

He made a gesture, a snap of his head, and tugged at the leash. Misha rose and together they marched off in the direction of the birches, the dog sniffing out the path ahead. Kira came out of the house and stood on the porch. Kharkovnakov stopped, looked at her briefly and continued walking. Soon he was only another shadow in the trees.

She came to the fence and stood where her husband had been, hands plunged into the pockets of her coat, her expression tense, strained.

"You shouldn't have come back here," she said and glanced around. "Everyone's gone. Only the two of us are left."

"Where's Nicholas?"

"Gone," she said as though she meant to imply something greater than distance.

"I have to talk to Nicholas," I said, pointing toward the birches. "Whatever your husband's done, whatever Nicholas has done, it has to be stopped."

"I can't help you, Mr. Hunter," she said.

"Kira—"

"No. You saw him. You must know that."

"Tell me where Nicholas is, that's all I need."

She shook her head. "I can't help you."

"Kira," I said, "you have to listen to me. They know

132

about the ikon—the Russians, the people in Washington. Everyone knows."

She listened impassively.

"They'll kill him if they have to," I said.

"You're asking me to betray my husband. I won't do that. Even if it means his death."

"I'm not asking you to betray him."

"Yes!" she said loudly. "Worse, you're asking me to betray the people who believe in him."

"Is it betrayal to save his life?"

"It's *his* life. Not yours. Not mine. What is done is done." She stopped and spoke again in a tired voice. "Would it be so hard for you just to walk away? Go back to your own life, Mr. Hunter. Leave us with ours."

"I can't, Kira."

"You don't even know who we are," she said. "You don't even know what's happened."

"I know someone's going to get hurt. Please, Kira, tell me where Nicholas is. If I can get to him, I can stop it. Let me try."

"Words," she said. "Words on top of words. What will you say to him? What will you tell our beloved priest?"

"That the world doesn't need another martyr."

"The world doesn't care," she said.

"But you do, Kira."

She came forward, and the sun caught her face.

"If I tell you where he is, will you leave us alone?"

"Yes," I said, another promise I wasn't certain I could keep.

"Nicholas has gone to New York," she said. "To church."

"Where, Kira? Where is the church?"

As she told me, her face revealed nothing. Whether it was an act of betrayal or one of redemption, I didn't know. I had the feeling she didn't know herself.

15

THE CHURCH WAS on the Upper West Side in the middle of a
block that was next on some developer's hit list. On either
side were empty buildings and a big blue sign proclaiming
that any minute "luxury condominiums" would begin to
sprout where these humble skeletons now stood. The
church wouldn't be far behind. Someone had written
"Fuck you, bozo" on the sign.

At one time, the street must have been filled with people
who survived on simple ideas that nobody had time for
anymore. Their sons and daughters now lived in Connecti-
cut and kicked themselves for not buying the old tenement
so they could sell it as a luxury condo. The ones who
wouldn't leave sat in small apartments with brown walls.
They didn't know from condominiums.

A rusty iron fence ran across the front of the church; the
gate was chained shut. So were the church doors at the top
of the steps. The building had once been white and there
were still traces of the color underneath the tall peaked
roof. At one time, the church must have had a name, too,
but it was covered in orange day-glow paint.

A steady trickle of worshipers entered through a side
door. They were mostly old. The men wore their ties stiffly,
self-consciously. The women walked behind them, heavy
boots around their thick ankles, brightly colored scarves
tied over their heads. At the door, they crossed themselves
as they entered and climbed the single flight of stairs to
the sanctuary.

It was a large church, and the high ceiling was covered
with angels floating across a powder-blue sky. A golden
archangel with a trumpet hovered in each corner. In the
center of the ceiling, dropping down from a billow of white

134

clouds, hung a huge brass chandelier that covered the room with a dim bronze light.

I stood in the back, under a scaffolding, and looked up. They were restoring the ceiling, and the back of the church was layered with a heavy film of grime that partially hid the angels and the huge enveloping clouds.

I looked for Nicholas but couldn't see him.

Most of the people stood. Those who couldn't sat in folding chairs around the edge of the scaffolding. I moved slowly through the crowd, feeling the warmth of their bodies and the smell of sweat mingled with heavy incense.

Stopping next to a small dark woman, I listened to her repetitive murmur of faith. She gazed up at the tiers of ikons and the supporting columns of red marble that rose toward the ceiling. Above it all was a gigantic gold crucifix. Even in the dim light, the figure's agonized features were clear.

A priest, dressed in a golden robe, stepped out of the side door, censer in hand, swinging it in a smoky arch across the chancel. From behind and above me, I heard the choir as they settled into the back balcony. The priest positioned himself on the steps leading down to the sanctuary and sang out a prayer.

Worshipers crossed themselves. A man in a dreary gray coat stared at me as I stepped in front of him. In the chancel, another priest opened the doors, exposing the altar. I walked slowly through the crowd, stepping across the front of the church.

I saw Nicholas standing on the far right side, looking anxiously toward the back of the church as if he expected someone.

He had become a different man. Dressed in a plain black cassock, lost in its dark folds, he seemed smaller, vulnerable. As I got closer, I could see his pale face and the beads of sweat that covered his forehead. He looked like a man who had made a final, irrevocable decision. He glanced quickly at his watch and brought his eyes to the front of the church, scanning the faces. When he came to mine, he was shocked, then stared in angry disbelief.

The choir echoed the priest's song. Nicholas crossed him-

135

self and tried to move away, but there was nowhere to go. The crowd blocked his escape.

"What are you doing here?" he whispered when I stood next to him.

"I could ask you the same thing."

He looked wildly around the sanctuary.

"How did you find me?"

"Kira told me," I said.

"Kira?" he said. "They were supposed to—" He stopped.

"What?"

He became suddenly composed. "It doesn't matter," he said. "Nothing matters. Leave, Hunter, you're too late."

"I came to make a deal."

"Then you're a fool."

"Would you rather talk to the police? I can't put you in jail; they can. Forget about the Russians or anybody from Washington. They'll only kill you. I can help you get out of it."

"You can't help anyone, Hunter. You can't even help yourself now."

"Whatever you're planning, call it off while there's still time. Give me the ikon."

"There is no ikon," Nicholas said.

"Yes there is," I said and took out the book. "How many have you stolen, Nicholas? For what? To keep Kharkovnakov's dreams alive a little longer?"

He grabbed for the book, but I put it away. "An even trade," I said. "The ikon for the book."

"Never."

"You don't understand, Nicholas," I said and took hold of his arm. "I'm not giving you the option."

"It's you who don't understand, Hunter. You weren't there when Stalin came to us before the Great War. Defend us, he said, for the love of God. For Mother Russia! They went, all of them—my father, my brother. Like sheep. My father was a priest, Hunter, in Leningrad. He died in one of his camps. Everyone died except me. I got out, I survived."

The voices around drained away. People began to stare. A woman gestured for silence.

136

"There will be no deals, Hunter," he whispered. "Not now, not ever."

"Is that what you kept the money for—survival?"

"It went to Kharkovnakov—all of it."

"No," I said, "the money you hid in the back of the ikon. They found it this morning."

"Oh, my God," he said. His arm began to move beneath the cassock and I tightened my grip, working my way down to his hand and the gun.

"I want the ikon, Nicholas."

"The ikon belongs to me—not to you or the Russians or to someone like Angle. It belongs only to the dead."

"Where is it?"

He shoved me away. I lost my balance and fell against the woman who had been staring at us. Nicholas pushed his way through the crowd, trying to get to the front of the church. People began shouting at me. I tried to reach for him, but someone grabbed me from behind, holding me back. As I shook him off, I saw Nicholas standing on the steps leading to the ikonostasis. He looked toward the back of the church and waved his hands.

I turned and saw her, standing near the entrance in a circle of light. Kimberly Wyeth saw me and turned toward the entrance. In seconds she was gone, lost in the crowds still coming into the church. I ran after her, but the crowd was too heavy. By the time I reached the street, she was nowhere in sight. I ran back to the jeep.

As I unlocked the door, Boris stepped out of the shadow of the building.

"Hunter," he said, pointing the gun at me, "please. Do not make a commotion. Get into the car." He was very calm about the whole thing. I stopped.

"Hunter," he said, "I would mourn your passing. But you would be dead in any event."

Everything inside me blew up.

"That does it," I said and threw the keys at his feet. "You want the car? Take the car. Take it! Stick the key in the ignition and run the son of a bitch into a wall. I'm sick of you people. I'm sick of people lying to me and sticking guns in my face and telling me what to do. I quit!"

Boris stepped back, stunned.

"You are upset with me," he said.

"Well, why not you?" I shouted. "You're in the right place. Something bad happens and here you are. So why not you?" The gun dropped a little in his hand. "Will you put the goddam gun away, Boris?" He put it in his pocket. I picked up the keys and sat down on the passenger seat.

"What the hell are you doing here anyway? What brings you out of your hole tonight?"

I expected anger, but there was only resignation.

"Nicholas," he said. "I was to meet him in the church. I changed my mind."

"You saw me."

"I saw Kimberly Wyeth," he said. "I thought I could wait. I took a walk."

"You know, she wanted me to kill you—you and Angle. The pair of you for fifty grand."

"A handsome offer," Boris said. "Did you accept?"

"I thought about it."

"Are you carrying a gun, Hunter?"

"Worried?"

"Curious."

"No."

"We have one gun between us. I think I will keep it with me."

"We don't have dirt between us, Boris," I said.

"I am sorry you feel that way."

"Stop it, Boris, your humility is making me nauseated." I pulled out the ledger book. "I found this in Nicholas' house. I can't read it, but there's a name that keeps popping up. Sort of like you, Boris. You'll jump right in if I'm getting anywhere, won't you?"

"Would it be too troublesome to continue our conversation inside?" he said. "I'm getting cold."

"Gosh, Boris, I'd hate to cause you any more trouble. That would be rude. Can I order you a pizza, something to tide you over?"

"That won't be necessary," he said and got into the jeep on the driver's side. He lit a cigarette and waited.

"Are you just going to sit there?"

"It is you who have so much to say, Hunter. Please, continue."

138

"Let's play twenty questions, okay?"

"I do not understand."

"I ask you a question and you give me a straight answer. You'll have to give up lying."

Boris sighed. "It is a little thing anyway."

"All right. You've been doing business with Nicholas—using Kimberly Wyeth as your sales agent."

"That is not a question, Hunter."

"You're right, Boris, just answer it."

"Yes, Nicholas and I have been doing business. I thought that was fairly obvious, even to you."

"How come you haven't got the Fyodor ikon?"

Boris shrugged. "I suppose Nicholas received a better offer than mine."

"You were waiting in the porn booth to pay him?"

"I knew something had happened when he did not arrive. It would come someday but I do not understand why it took him so long."

"Maybe it was Kimberly's idea. Maybe she got tired of being the middleman and went directly to the source. Where did Nicholas get the ikons he sold to you?"

"I never asked him. It was not my concern."

"You ought to teach at Harvard Business School," I said. "You'd fit right in. Why did Nicholas want to see you tonight?"

"Now I think he wanted to kill me. Perhaps he asked Kimberly to help him. My disappearance would solve many problems."

"Where is Kimberly now?"

"Angle's, I think. That is where she will be."

"If I were Kimberly Wyeth, I'd be out of the country."

"That is not possible, I'm afraid. I have men assigned to watch the airport and her apartment building. She is not entirely stupid. Who else can she turn to but Angle?"

"Would she go to Hermitage?"

"I know her, Hunter. She feels threatened. She acts irrationally. Perhaps it was she who wanted to kill us, the priest and myself. Where is Nicholas?"

"He ran away."

Boris nodded. "Then, she will go to the one place she has left."

"So, who's got the ikon, Boris?"

"I think Martin Angle. He has a need for such things and he has the money. It would seem logical."

"I gave up logic years ago," I said. "What if you have it, Boris? What if you only wanted to get rid of Kimberly? Aside from Nicholas, she's the only one who knows your business. Why not get rid of both of them?" I snapped my fingers. "I know just the spot—a church. Nobody would think of that."

"I do business with them, Hunter. I do not kill my business. Kimberly, perhaps, but not Nicholas. She also works for Angle. Perhaps she works for others as well—people in your own government?"

"Our government doesn't steal ikons," I said.

"Who was the man who spoke to you in the coffee shop? You think I do not know about that? Or the other ones who spoke to you? Did you think they were doing this because they are such great patriots?"

"No," I said, "they're in it for the money, like all the rest of you."

"They have a perfect cover," Boris said. "If anyone asks why, they can say, 'We are fighting the Russians.' Americans do not discriminate when it comes to us. We are all bad. They want a part of the business, Hunter. I know this. If someone is hurt, they can accuse me or even Kharkovnakov. He is not a citizen of your country. He stays because it would be embarrassing to ask him to leave. But this, stealing, this would allow them to move against him with total justification."

Conshocken would be happy with that, I thought.

"Listen to me, Hunter," Boris said. "There is another possibility—that Kimberly Wyeth does some work for the same people who came to see you. She has money, she flies here and there. She meets interesting people. Her behavior overseas would be well known to them. So, they make a deal with her. They set her up to get the ikon and give it to them. They are now in business." Boris smiled at his own cleverness. "Of course, you and I are dead but we are much more easily disposed of than the daughter of an American Secretary of State."

"He's dead, too. How do you explain me?"

140

Boris rolled down the window and tossed his cigarette into the street. "You are the wild card," he said. "Perhaps they even know you are coming here. Who told you about the church?"

"Kharkovnakov's wife. Who does she work for?"

"Perhaps she is innocent."

"How did you know somebody came to see me?"

"I had you followed. You are interesting to me."

"Did you send somebody to my house?"

"No," he said and hesitated. "Only to the lawyer's office. She is more than just your lawyer, I think."

"You're such a liar, Boris."

"No," he said. Again, he hesitated. "I am not lying."

"Then what's your problem?"

"I was not the only one who spied on you. There were others, but I am not certain who they were. My men did not see clearly."

"You really are a son of a bitch, you know that, Boris?"

"Do you believe me?"

"I wouldn't believe you if you parted the Red Sea. What do you want with the ikon, aside from the money? Can't forget about the money."

"I want it for my own reasons," he said.

"Not good enough, Boris."

"You are being difficult."

"Not half as difficult as I could be. I want you to keep that in mind."

"All right," he said. "Angle will try to use the ikon to further his ties with us. You know the current situation. Many people are waiting to see what will happen. There is a great struggle going on, people fighting for power. Some of them would like to see Angle succeed. Others would not. The reasons are irrational, but that is unimportant. In a storm, people grab anything they think will save them."

"But if Angle has the ikon, you'll have to offer him something. You don't have the money to buy it back."

"True," he said and thought about it. "I could offer to remove Kimberly for him. I think he finds her as distasteful as I do. If I had the ikon, I would be in a position to offer him many things. An interesting friendship, yes?"

"I find it hard to believe you have any friends, Boris."

He lit another cigarette and rubbed his eyes. "I will tell you something, Hunter. I was born in Moscow. Three families in four rooms. We stood in line for the bathroom. We waited for the kitchen. We are a nation of lines. I do not stand in line any longer. That has nothing to do with ideology."

"It has to do with greed," I said.

"But I am happy, you see? I have my life, and I think that is enough. So many do not have even that. This bothers you. I see that. Next you will ask me what I believe in."

"What do you believe in, Boris? Marx? Lenin? Onward and upward with the dialectic? What?"

He laughed. "What do I really believe in? What am I to do with my life? What are my goals? Such questions, Hunter, so many choices, so much to do. How can you Americans carry so many things around with you all the time? I am mystified, really I am."

"You still haven't answered the question."

"I do not stand in line, that is my goal. I have done that. As for the rest, Hunter, my life is for living. When it is over, I will stand in another line behind Stalin and Brezhnev."

He rolled down the window and blew cigarette smoke into the cold night air.

"How many people have you killed, Boris?"

"Not many," he said. "Enough. You?"

"Enough," I said.

He took a long drag and flipped the cigarette away. "Then perhaps we are not so different, Hunter."

"Yes, we are."

He rolled up the window. "Then you have a chance to make a choice. You can go with me or you can stay. But you must make the choice."

"Where are you going?"

"Angle's, of course."

"What are you going to do if I decide to pass?"

"I will steal your jeep," he said, "with your permission."

"There's something I have to do first."

"What?"

"I want to call Jamie," I said.

Boris rubbed the steering wheel and sighed.

"We do not have the luxury of time at the moment," he said quietly and without looking at me. "I do not know what we will find at Martin Angle's. Perhaps the Americans will be there before us. If so, we can go home to our warm beds, Hunter. But there is not time now. Make your choice, decide."

"Shit," I said.

"Yes?" Boris said and started the jeep. He drove quickly through the streets, his eyes on the traffic ahead of us.

"You must be very much in love," he said.

"Yes," I said.

He shook his head. "Then I feel very sorry for you, Hunter."

I took it as a joke and laughed.

16

I WANTED to call in an air strike, but Boris had another idea.

The plan was simple. Boris would stagger to the front door and act like a disgusting foreign drunk. Unable to contain his condescension, the doorman would tell Boris to fuck off. Boris would pretend to throw up on the doorman, who would back away in fear and loathing at the idea of Slavic vomit on his lapel. Boris would stumble into the building and promptly smack the doorman, who would then be decent enough to fall down. I would follow immediately and the two of us would drag the now unconscious body of the doorman into the bathroom, tie him up with whatever we could find and emerge from the toilet triumphant.

It went approximately like that except Boris had to hit the doorman twice before he dropped. Boris picked him up under the arms and I grabbed his legs and we swung him into the bathroom. We tied him up with some twine from his desk drawer. Boris studied the console.

"Do you understand these things?"

"More or less," I said. I took an educated guess and pressed a button or two, and the elevator door slid open. When we got inside, Boris screwed a long silencer on the barrel of his gun.

"How are you feeling, Hunter?"

"To tell you the truth, I'm scared to death."

Boris looked mildly amused. "Here," he said, handing me a small gun.

"You said you only had one."

"I lied," he said.

The elevator rose toward the fifth floor. We watched the numbers.

"I hope you're good at this," I said as we passed four.

Boris smiled. "Stand over there, away from the door."

The elevator stopped, and he held the door closed for ten minutes. He released it and flattened against the side of the elevator. The door jerked open onto an empty hallway. Boris waited, tapping his foot anxiously on the floor.

"Nobody home," I said.

"It would seem so."

"What are we waiting for?"

"Nothing," he said.

We went from room to room, but all of them were empty. We pushed through the doors of the library, but it was empty as well. Angle had disappeared.

"They could be anywhere in the building," I said. "They might not even be here."

"Don't think where they might be," he said. "Think where they will be."

"The gallery."

"I think we should go in from the bottom," I said.

Boris pointed at the elevator. "Down?"

We descended to the lobby again and searched the doorman for keys, finding a set in a small plastic pouch strapped to his leg. We unlocked the door on the other side of the lobby and walked down a narrow unlit hallway toward the floor of the gallery. I looked through the window in the door.

"Nobody home," I said. The statue in the middle of the gallery was still bathed in cool light, and the stream flowed around her feet. I pressed my ear against the glass and heard the sound of music.

Boris inserted a key in the door, then another. Finally, one turned and he opened the door. The music was loud, booming throughout the gallery. We stepped inside and moved toward one of the corners.

"Have you got a plan, Boris?" I asked over the music.

"No."

"You're the spy."

"We must find out what is going on upstairs," he said. "We do not go together."

"I don't think I like your plan very much."

"One goes, one stays," he said. "If they are here and it is

a trap, both are not caught." He reached in his pocket and took out a silver dollar. "For good luck," he said and gave it to me. "Heads I go, tails you go."

I tossed the coin in the air and turned it over on the back of my hand. I looked through my fingers.

Tails. Shit.

Boris stayed in the corner while I made my way slowly up the ramp. The music, blasting out of the ceiling speakers, grew louder as I moved up. I kept my eyes locked on the top railing,. wondering if Kimberly or even Angle would suddenly lean over the edge and shoot me. I had made the final turn when I heard a shot and flattened out on the ramp. Then I heard something that sounded like laughter and another shot and I rolled as fast as I could against the wall. The gun in my hand felt very small. I told myself I'd feel a lot more secure with a grenade launcher.

I inched forward and the top floor came into view. By that time, it was fairly easy to see what was going on. Any fool could have figured it out. Angle and the Mormon were tied up underneath the row of ikons. Angle was bleeding from several small cuts on his face, and there were several holes in the wall directly over his head. His teeth were clenched together in terror and he was crying. The Mormon was slumped over on the floor, either dead or passed out.

Kimberly stood a dozen feet in front of him, laughed and took another shot at him. The bullet missed his head by six inches.

I crawled up a few more feet and slipped into the doorway on the fifth floor. Kimberly stepped back toward the railing and sat down, laying the gun next to her on the floor. She pulled out a small bottle from her coat, opened it, poured a mound of white powder on the back of her hand and snorted it. Catching the rush, she shook her head back and forth and swallowed hard. Kimberly was wired to the gills.

Angle tried to move, and she grabbed the gun and racked off another shot. It went wild, punching a hole in one of the ikons. She got a real chuckle out of that and pumped another one into the picture.

Time to leave, I thought and made my way back down to Boris.

"She's up there," I said. "Stoned out of her mind and taking potshots at Angle."

Boris managed a thin smile. "How is Mr. Angle taking all this?"

"Not well. He's tied up."

Boris checked his gun.

"No," I said.

"We have no choice."

"Yes, we do."

I watched while Boris climbed up the ramp. He slipped inside the doorway and waited. I stepped into the center of the first floor and stood next to the statue of Diana. Then I yelled Kimberly's name as loud as I could.

Nothing happened. I stepped away from the statue and yelled again, repeating her name several times.

Kimberly popped up over the edge of the railing and shot at me. The bullet smacked into the statue, decapitating one pure alabaster breast. I threw myself down behind Diana and another shot splashed into the stream.

I looked up to see Kimberly moving along the railing, keeping one hand on it to steady herself. I could see her mouth moving, yelling something as she moved down the railing past the doorway. Boris stepped out and kicked her legs out from under her. She flew forward, tumbling downward to the next level. When she stopped, she curled up in a ball and lay still. Boris ran after her and kicked the gun over the railing. I followed it down through the trees and the light, watching it turn and twist all the way down. Then I climbed up the ramp to meet him. Together, we dragged her to the top.

"The first thing we're going to do is turn off this goddam music," I yelled. Boris nodded. We dropped Kimberly and I went looking for the switch. Angle stared at us, his face white with fear.

"I want to shut this off!" I yelled at him, and he nodded weakly toward a side door. I opened it and found the controls.

The music stopped abruptly. In the silence, the only

147

thing I could hear was the pathetic sound of Angle's sobbing.

"You can come up with the next plan," I said.

"This one wasn't so bad, Hunter," Boris said and raised the gun in Angle's direction.

I crossed in front of his aim and knelt down. Angle whispered harshly, "Kill him! Kill both of them!"

I put my hand around his throat and squeezed. "Shut up," I said politely. I looked back at Boris.

"How badly is he hurt?" Boris asked.

I relaxed my hand and looked at Angle's face. His bulging eyes followed mine.

"He'll live," I said.

"Then we should let him bleed a little more. It must be quite a new experience for him."

I stood up. "You had me worried for a moment."

"For a moment," he said, "I was worried about myself as well."

"How's Kimberly?"

"She will live as well. Why don't we untie Mr. Angle and his friend? They appear to be extremely uncomfortable."

I untied the Mormon first. After a few minutes, he opened his eyes and looked around.

"Your job still having its moments?" I asked.

"I'm quitting," he said. "I mean it this time."

I untied Angle, and he sat rubbing his wrists. Boris took the flask out of his pocket and tossed it at him. Angle ducked and covered his head. The flask landed in his lap. He stared at it for a moment, then opened it and gulped half of it down.

When he stopped coughing, he took another long drink. The flask shook in his hands, and when he finished, his hands were still trembling.

"Are you going to kill me? he asked.

"No," Boris said. "You're much too important to kill." He waved his arms, gesturing expansively. "You are my country's great friend. We do not shoot our friends." He paused. "Unless they become awkward, of course."

"I need another drink," Angle said. He looked as if he was going to need an endless supply. "She wanted to kill

148

me," he said incredulously, as though it had occurred to someone else. His voice was edgy with hysteria.

"We saved your life, I'm sorry to say."

Boris stepped forward and took the flask. He wiped the top with his hand and took a drink. He got one small gulp and turned the flask upside down.

"Pig," Boris said. "The pig drank it all."

Kimberly started to come around. She stood up slowly, climbing the railing, twitching as she moved. When she finally made it, she held her arm.

"It hurts," she said, looking plaintively at us.

I didn't see it coming. Angle pushed himself off the wall and staggered toward her, gaining momentum as he moved. Boris dropped the flask and twisted toward him, bringing the gun up. I took three steps and leaped at Angle. He picked her up by her legs and flipped her over the railing. I hit him and we both rolled toward the edge.

I stopped, but Angle slipped halfway over the edge before he could grab the railing. Kimberly never screamed. She fell silently, turning over once before she landed face first across the stream. One arm flopped spastically and splashed into the water.

Everything was quiet for a moment, then the Mormon said, "Jesus."

Boris stepped over to the railing and turned Angle over on his back, his head and shoulders dangling over the edge. Boris put his foot in the middle of Angle's stomach and aimed the long silencer at his face. His eyes moved slowly to mine, a clinical stare, like a scientist waiting to see if the specimen would make it through the experiment.

I stared back, but his eyes gave nothing away. I had the feeling that if I peeled back his skin, layer by layer, that if I could get inside his skull, I would find a dark empty plain filled with phantoms.

The moment passed. He lowered the gun, stuck it in his coat pocket and hauled Angle back on the floor. Angle leaned against one of the railing posts.

"You are becoming very awkward," Boris said to him. "Now tell me where I can find the ikon." Angle pointed toward the door where the music controls were.

"Thank you," Boris said. "Watch him very carefully, Hunter."

I looked down once more at Kimberly and then at Angle. The Mormon was still sitting against the wall.

"I think there's an opportunity here for you," I said to the Mormon. He looked at me blankly and then something very close to recognition emerged in his eyes.

"It's a thought," he said, smiling at Angle.

Boris stepped out of the door, carrying a small, nearly black ikon. He held it out for me. There was only the vaguest hint of an image on it, the dark outline of a face. Near the bottom, one hand, a ghostly white, had been saved. In the light it seemed to glow.

Boris turned the ikon around and began examining it. He pulled it close to his eye and looked at it. He rubbed the wood between his fingers, turned it over and looked at the back. Then he began to laugh.

Angle said, "What?"

"It is a fake," Boris said, laughing louder. "An excellent one. But a fake."

"You're lying," Angle said. "I paid for it." He looked at me. "He's lying."

"How would you know?" I said. "You just buy them. Are you lying, Boris?"

"Absolutely not," he said. "Nicholas has played us all for fools."

"Where's the real one?"

"I do not know."

"Is there a real one?"

"At the moment," Boris said, "there seems to be some doubt about that."

Angle said, "He's got it, Hunter."

It was a reasonable assumption, I thought.

"Would you do something sneaky like that, Boris? Stage this whole thing just to get in good with what's-his-name over here? You wouldn't do something as potentially rotten as that, would you?"

"No," Boris said, not laughing any longer.

"I'm not sure I believe that."

"I wish I had thought of it, Hunter."

150

"You know something, Boris," I said. "I can see it. Where is it? Where's the real ikon?"

"If it exists, Nicholas has it. Zemlya."

I looked around at everything, at Boris and Angle and the Mormon sitting in the back with a cheesy smile on his face. I glanced over the railing at Kimberly. The water had soaked through her dress. I could just see it rippling as the stream swept past her legs.

"I'm going to make a phone call and then I'm going to leave you to yourselves," I said.

"Shoot him, Hunter," Angle said. "Kill him. I'll pay you for it."

"There you are, Hunter," Boris said. "You have an excellent incentive. Money. The American dream.

"I'm getting awfully sick of this," I said.

"Shoot him, Hunter," Angle yelled. "Shoot the bastard!"

"Who *are* you going to shoot, Hunter?" Boris said. He still hadn't taken the gun out of his pocket.

"He's a fucking Russian!" Angle yelled.

I stuck my gun in his face. "I know who he is. Now I want you to shut up."

Boris started to say something.

"Why don't you shut the fuck up, too," I said.

I turned back to Angle. "What were you going to do with the ikon?"

"Some people came by," he said.

"Conshocken?"

"That's the one," the Mormon said.

"Tell me what they said."

Angle answered. "I told them I didn't have it. They wanted to know if I was interested in buying any more."

"Did they believe you?"

"I don't know," he said, pointing at the place where Kimberly had gone over. "She wanted it, she said she wanted it!"

"She's dead," I said. "What are you going to do, Boris?"

"You have the gun," he said.

"I resign," I said and threw it to him. I walked away, heading for the door into the other building.

151

"Hunter," Boris said quietly. Then, "Never mind. Go make your phone call. I'll be here."

"You're going to leave me with him?" Angle yelled.

"You bet," I said.

I sat down at Angle's desk and closed my eyes. All I could see was Kimberly's body. I called Jamie at home, but there was no answer, so I tried her office.

"She hasn't come back yet, Hunter," her secretary said.

"Did she call?"

"No, but it's all right."

Something was wrong.

"What do you mean, it's all right?"

"She's with Kira," she said. "Right after you called this morning, Kira called. Jamie had told me about her, so I gave her the number."

She kept talking, but I couldn't understand what she was saying. I hung the phone up slowly and collapsed back in the chair.

"Jamie?" I said and looked up. Boris was standing in the doorway.

"They took her this morning," he said. "Two of Kharkovnakov's people. Believe me, I would have stopped it if I could."

"Where is she?"

"Zemlya," he said. I tried to raise my arms. They seemed too heavy to move.

"You knew at the church."

"One of my men saw them this morning. If you had known you would not have helped me. I needed your help."

"Why?" I screamed at him. The sound seemed to blow him back against the door.

"Nicholas wanted *you*, Hunter. She took your place."

"Kira knew."

"Yes, she must have."

"Kira won't hurt her," I said.

"I do not know," Boris said. "But Nicholas is very desperate at the moment."

"What will he do?"

"Perhaps he will try to make a deal with the Americans. The real ikon is all he has left to bargain with."

"He's got Jamie."

152

"The Americans do not care about your friend. I suspect they are on their way to Zemlya now."

"You could have stopped them this morning, Boris."

"No, Hunter."

"You could have stopped it, you son of a bitch!"

"I cannot change what happened. We are the only chance she has now."

I was swept away by a peculiar fantasy. I saw it happen, saw her death in my mind, watched it helplessly. I was there, standing empty-handed at the grave. I saw my life as it would be without her.

"I should have shot you when I had the opportunity," I said.

Boris said nothing.

"I don't want her to die," I said, using the word for the first time. It sounded cold and precise in the empty room. "I don't want anything to happen to her."

Boris stared at me sadly, keeping whatever he knew or felt inside.

We left Angle and the Mormon to clean up the mess in the gallery and took the elevator down to the first floor. Boris lit a cigarette and stared through the smoke at the carpet.

"Did Nicholas tell you about his family?" he asked.

"He said they died."

"He informed on them," Boris said.

"He what?"

"Haven't you wondered why a priest would do business with me, Hunter?"

"You blackmailed him?"

Boris shrugged. "Kharkovnakov needed money to fight his holy war. It was a marriage of convenience. I found out about Nicholas two years ago. The moment I met him I knew something was wrong. Do you ever have those feelings?"

I didn't answer.

"It does not matter," Boris said. "He was almost relieved when I told him."

As the doors opened, Boris said, "Do you know what he told me when I asked him why he became a priest?"

"I don't give a damn, Boris."

He didn't say any more. I carried the ikon between us like a wall.

17

WE GOT IN the jeep and headed across town to the West Side Drive and then up to the George Washington Bridge. As we came out onto the bridge, I thought of the times Jamie and I had driven across it. She said it always reminded her of the first time she'd even been to New York. Everywhere I looked, I saw her again. What a horrible surprise, I thought. When we crossed back into New Jersey, Boris spoke.

"I hope she is alive, Hunter."

"She's alive. I want you to keep thinking that."

"I did not anticipate any of these complications," he said. "It was simply a business arrangement."

"Is that your excuse? What the hell did you expect?"

He lapsed into silence. I drove fast, not really caring about the police. After a few miles, I slowed down to sixty-five and kept it steady.

"A business arrangement," I said. "Jesus Christ. You lie, you blackmail people, you shoot them and then you sit back and tell yourself how terribly clever you are. And then you complain about complications."

"Please," he said, "let us not talk about my morality any longer. I suppose your Mr. Conshocken's ideals are more congenial?"

"You're all the same, Boris. Who's bright idea was it to use Kimberly?"

"Our people in Rome passed her to me. As pathetic as she was, they thought she might be of some use."

"You probably couldn't wait to get your hands on her."

"I take what is offered to me," he said. "I make no excuses."

"What about Dimitri? Was he pathetic enough for you?"

Boris looked surprised. "Our famous spy? No, I am

155

afraid Dimitri was merely greedy and very stupid. Even the Russians in Hermitage did not want him."

"But you did, Boris."

"Dimitri came to us," he said. "He had no friends, no money. It seemed a great opportunity. Suddenly, the FBI had a Russian spy who filled their ears with tales of espionage. I think we played him very well. The Americans offered to trade him, but we told them we did not want him. They were very upset, furious." He stopped talking and looked at me. "It is the way things are done in the world, Hunter."

"Don't give me a lecture on reality. Our old men threaten your old men and nobody even knows what they're fighting for anymore. That's reality, Boris. Or money, that's your reality."

"What do you fight for, Hunter? Words on paper?"

"I'm fighting to save somebody I love. It's the only reason that makes any sense."

"Then you are a lucky man," he said. "Like your country."

"How the hell would you know, Boris?"

"I know what I am, Hunter. And I know what you are. Perhaps that is why I am here." He lit a cigarette and cracked the window, watching the smoke slip out of the jeep in a thin curved stream.

"You wouldn't know the truth if it sat up and talked, Boris."

"I did not have to tell you about your friend, Hunter. I could have given you the fake and let you go."

"Hell," I said, "you probably don't even know why you told me."

Boris laughed. "You're right, Hunter, I do not really know. I know that I am a realist. Like the people in the cemetery. They are very realistic. Even the old general, asleep under the stone. I would have liked to meet him, talk to him. To fight so hard, to lose so much. That must change a man."

"Maybe you'll still get your chance," I said.

We drove for a long while without speaking.

"Why haven't you defected, Boris?"

156

"I have thought about it," he said seriously. "I cannot go to embassy parties for the rest of my life."

"You could buy your house on Long Island."

"I hate Long Island. I would like to live out west. The Sunbelt."

"By the way, Boris, did you know that the ikon was a fake before we went to Angle's?"

"Of course not," he said stiffly.

"Jesus," I said. "You can't stop, can you?"

He shrugged his shoulders and smiled. "It is my nature," he said.

Up ahead, the road to Hermitage.

And Jamie.

As we drove down the two-lane road, it began to snow, soft heavy flakes. Boris took his gun out and removed the silencer.

"Park at the church," he said.

"It'll take too long to walk."

"Would you prefer we drove up to Zemlya and gave everyone the opportunity to know we are coming? Park at the church."

I followed the road as it wound along the mountain. I kept repeating a phrase to myself, one that had been with me ever since New York. I would find Jamie and she would be all right. I knew that saying it wouldn't do any good. But it kept me from screaming out loud.

The church was deserted. The wind pushed the fresh snow through the cemetery and around the car. Boris checked his gun, pulling out the clip, ramming it back.

"Your gun will not be much good from a distance," he said.

"I hope I don't have to use it."

He gave me that sad smile of his. "I hope so, too. Check it, please."

I took it out and spun the small cylinder, hearing it click.

"When this is over, Hunter, we will have dinner together, you and I and your friend. I know a place. Very good clams."

"Are you paying?"

"Naturally," he said.

We got out of the car and walked across the parking lot and into the field, stepping into snow that was up to my calves. We slogged through it, staying out of the road.

"Do you consider yourself a patriot, Hunter?" Boris asked.

"Only by degree," I said, and he laughed.

We stayed in the field until the bridge and crossed into the road. Zemlya was barely visible, a bright white fan of light in the falling snow. Boris touched my shoulder.

"Into the ditch," he whispered.

"What?"

"Go," he said and shoved me down. I heard the sound of someone coming down the road, jogging at half speed. The sound stopped and started again. Footsteps thumped over the bridge. Boris put his finger to his mouth. The footsteps left the bridge and stopped in front of us.

Through the snow, I saw a dark figure standing in the road. Boris jumped out of the ditch and knocked him down. I scrambled up after him. The man lay spread-eagled on his back across the road. Boris lit a match and held it over him.

"You didn't have to do that, Hunter," Samuels said.

"I didn't. Boris did."

"You're Strinsky," Samuels said.

"Roll over," Boris said.

"What're you going to do?"

"Are you going to argue with him?" I said.

"Nope," Samuels said and rolled over. Boris searched him and found his gun. He gave it to me.

"I'm a regular arsenal now," I said. Samuels sat up, rubbing his knees.

"Where's the rest of you?" I said.

"Conshocken and the other guy are up there," he said, pointing at Zemlya.

"Where's Jamie?"

"That your lawyer?" Samuels said. "Beats me."

"Right," I said. "Stand up."

Samuels got to his feet. "I was supposed to keep an eye on you. I lost you in Jersey."

"What are they doing up there?" Boris said.

158

"I don't know," Samuels said. "Waiting?"

"Then we should not keep them too long," Boris said.

"You can be our tour guide," I said, pushing Samuels along.

We moved back to the field, punching through heavy snow to the thatch of dead grass underneath. We kept in single file, Samuels between us.

"You don't seem dumb enough to be working with Conshocken," I said to him.

"It's a long story."

"How much are you getting paid again?"

"Not enough," Samuels said.

"I remember. If you yell when we get up there, Boris will probably shoot you. It might only be your leg, but I can't guarantee it."

"No problem," Samuels said. "When this is over, I'm moving back to Florida. Ever since he started on this thing, Ed's been kind of rabid, you know? I think he feels he's been underpaid."

"He struck me as a tedious son of a bitch. Who's the other one?"

"He said his name was Jones. I told him if he's Jones, I'm Ernest Hemingway. He liked that."

"You should see him perform in a Chock Full o' Nuts. Is he one of you guys?"

"How can you tell these days?" Samuels said. "Your lawyer, she a friend of yours?"

"Yes," I said. "Nicholas kidnapped her this morning."

Samuels whistled. "I hope she wasn't a close friend," he said.

I almost hit him for that.

Zemlya was above us, the light shimmering through the snow, setting off tiny rainbows that died the moment they were born.

"I do not like going in through the gate," Boris said. He looked at Samuels. "Where are your friends?"

"I don't know."

"Is there a way in through the birches? Up the other side?" I asked.

"Can you climb a mountain?"

"Hardly."

"Then we go in through the gate," Boris said.

"Let Samuels go first," I said. His mouth opened and closed rapidly. "They're your friends," I said.

We climbed up the road to Zemlya, walking in the snow-covered tire tracks.

Boris kept walking. At the first turn, he stopped and leaned against the rocks in the shelter of the high wall of stone. He took out his flask and put it to his lips.

"It's empty," I said. He tossed it in the road. Then he reached out to catch the falling snow. "Quite beautiful," he said. "Like a dream."

We continued up the road underneath the soft umbrella of light. Samuels was out in front, the point man. Boris and I stayed back, spread out on either side like the base of an invisible triangle. We walked slowly, following the twists in the road. At the last turn before the gate, we stopped.

"Good luck, my friend," Boris said. "I hope you find her. Stay close to the rocks. Don't make yourself a target."

As we pushed Samuels ahead of us around the corner, a pair of bright-yellow headlights came on. Two figures, each holding a rifle, waited on either side of the lights. Everyone stopped.

"Hey," Samuels said. "It's me."

"Get the hell out of the way," Conshocken said.

"Stay right where you are, Samuels," I told him.

"Well, make up your fucking minds," he said.

"I want the ikon," Conshocken said.

"Haven't got it, Ed."

"Don't give me that, Hunter. I want the goddam ikon."

"It's up there," I said.

"There's nothing up there. The place is locked."

"Hey, Jones," I said.

"Yeah?"

"Is he telling the truth?"

"Sure," Jones said. "He had to blow up the dog. Big son of a bitch tried to bite him. That right, Ed?"

"Shut up," Conshocken said.

"Say what, Ed?" Jones said.

160

Conshocken moved closer to the other agent, crossing the headlights.

"Shut up!" Conshocken yelled. "Strinsky?"

"Yes," Boris said.

"Where's the ikon?"

"I suppose it is where Hunter said it is."

Conshocken raised the rifle. "Tell me where it is or I'll blow your fucking head off!"

Boris shook his head and said, "I do not know."

I took a step forward.

"Hey, Ed," Jones said, and Conshocken turned slightly. Jones swung the rifle butt around and hit Conshocken in the middle of his face. His feet flew out from underneath him and he bounced back against the hood of the car, then fell face first in the snow. Jones bent down and yanked his head up by the hair.

"He's leaking all over the damn place," Jones said. He wiped his hands off in the snow. "Hello, Gregor," he said to Boris.

Boris reached in his pocket and gave Jones his gun.

"You know," Jones said, "I busted a guy's nose in training. Bastard didn't know how to set it. Doctor said it was going to look like dried shit all his life. How you doing, Hunter?"

"I'm in a hurry," I said.

"I can see that," he said and picked up Conshocken's rifle, tossing it to Samuels. "See you finally made it, shithead. Put Gregor in the car and try not to trip over anything."

"I took your advice, Hunter," Boris said.

"You're defecting?"

Jones laughed. "Fucking amateurs," he said. "Go on, Hunter, do whatever you got to do." I didn't move for a second. "Hey," he said, "show's over. The good guys won."

Lucky us, I thought and ran for the gate. They were wide open. Misha lay against the fence, her paws scraping slowly on the ground. There was blood on her muzzle. She looked up mutely as I ran past.

Spotlights lit up the house, breaking through the birches. I stood between the house and the trees and listened. The wind washed down from the mountain in heavy

161

clouds of snow that broke against the top of the trees and scattered. From the center of the birches I heard a scream.

I walked down the path toward the clearing. When I got close, I cut through the trees, coming out a few yards to the left of the path. There was a body in the middle of the clearing, kneeling in the snow.

Nicholas heard me and raised his head. I kept the gun out in front of me. I had the feeling he wanted me to shoot him. The flesh around his eyes was white and bloodless. He shivered as the black cassock swirled around him in the wind.

"Where is she?" I said, lowering the gun.

He raised a hand toward the house. I stepped away and ran toward the path. He screamed my name. I kept running. He screamed again and his voice followed me. It rose over the trees until it was lost in the emptiness of the sky.

The front door was locked, so I stepped back and fired three shots into the lock. Wood splattered and the doorknob split and dropped into the snow. I pushed it open slowly.

The front room was dark except for a red glow coming from the far corner. A dozen candles in red glass burned beneath a small ikon. I fumbled along the wall until I found the switch. It didn't work.

I didn't notice it until I touched the ikon. The face had been slashed, cut to pieces. I stepped away from it, terrified. I consciously slowed myself down, fighting panic. Jamie was here somewhere. Standing next to that ikon, I was suddenly afraid of finding her.

The door on my left led to the part of the house nearest the birches. I took a candle and began to search for her.

Behind the door was a short flight of stairs. At the top of the stairs was a hallway with three doors, one at the very end. I stepped into the hall and the end door slammed shut. The candle fell from my hand and banged on the floor as I flattened against the wall.

The air grew increasingly colder as I got closer to the door. My legs moved me forward faster, until I was taking the last few feet at a dead run, smashing into the door full force. It flew open and I dove inside, rolling over, gun up, straining to keep it from shaking too much.

162

The room was empty. Red shadows danced in the far corner under another ikon, the face slashed. Cold air blew into the room from an open window on the side.

In each of the other rooms it was the same—empty, except for another desecrated ikon. I stood looking at the face on the ikon and the walls began to close inward with the inexorable logic of a nightmare. I grabbed another candle and made my way down the stairs.

I walked back through the front room and through a doorway on the opposite side. I held the candle over my head as I went, the flame throwing petals of light across the ceiling.

The room was like all the others. A single candle burned on the top of a small corner table directly below another disfigured ikon. Whoever had slashed the ikon had left one eye intact. It seemed to stare across the room to another door.

Jamie.

If I found her in the room, I wouldn't scream. I wouldn't do anything except walk over to find out if she was still alive. If she wasn't, I'd go out and kill Nicholas and the others. I'd find Kharkovnakov and kill him, too. It was all very rational and completely insane. I repeated their names until they became meaningless sound, a mad prayer. I pushed open the door.

An ikon of the Virgin watched me from her corner, pristine and untouched. Sadness lay like a veil across her face. Jamie was on the floor beneath the ikon. Her hands lay on her knees, palms open. I stopped, waited, and held out the candle toward her still figure.

Jamie was crying.

I knelt down and pulled her toward me, surrounding her completely as she sobbed, smashing her hands helplessly against my chest. She raised her head, tried to speak, choked out my name and buried herself in my coat.

"Jamie?"

She wiped off her face and leaned against the wall.

"We have to find them, Jamie."

"You don't know what he looked like at the end," she said.

163

We went to find Kharkovnakov and his wife. I had no hope at all.

We found the entrance to the basement in Kharkovnakov's study, hidden underneath a rug. The study was a windowless room in the back of the house, the walls covered with paintings and ikons. I touched one of the ikons, and the paint came off in my hand, moist, chalky. There were other ikons stacked in one corner. I knew where Nicholas had gotten the ikons to sell.

The paintings were different, beautifully detailed scenes of of old Russia, some with the clarity of photographs. A fresh canvas sat clamped to an easel that had fallen over. I straightened it and glanced at the picture; a winter scene, set in a birch forest, not much different from the one that lay just behind the house.

Behind me, Jamie said, "He wanted to go home so badly."

I pulled on the metal hook and lifted the heavy wooden door. Below us, stone steps curved away. I pointed the gun into the darkness.

"I know her," Jamie said. "Let me go first."

She started down the stairs before I could stop her. I followed, the gun pointed over her shoulder at whatever was ahead of us. The stairs curved left into a short tunnel. The walls were stone. Every few feet a candle burned in a small holder, and above each was a bronze cross embedded in the stone.

The door at the end of the tunnel was open slightly, and the smell of incense poured through the opening. Our steps crackled on the cold floor. Jamie pushed the door open.

Inside was a church.

Straight ahead, Kharkovnakov knelt on the floor in front of the ikonostasis, surrounded by a circle of candles. Everywhere in the room, candles burned, sending out ribbons of light. I saw half a dozen people standing silently on the other side. Jamie put her hand on my arm.

Kira stepped out of the darkness. Jamie went to her. They spoke quietly, Kira nodding slowly. When they finished, they embraced, clinging tightly to one another in some secret grief.

164

Khrakovnakov hadn't moved. His huge body was stiff and erect, head bent back to stare up at the ikons in front of him. Above the golden doors was a small black ikon. His eyes were fixed on it. Jamie came back to me.

"She wants you to take it, the one you've been looking for."

I crossed the sanctuary to where Kharkovnakov knelt. As I pulled it down, I saw that the face was smeared with blood. I turned to look at him. In the glow of the candles, his body seemed on fire, and I saw his hands for the first time. They lay open at his sides, bloody and slashed. He had mutilated himself.

Then I saw his face.

He stared through me, his eyes black and empty, fixed on some distant place, some other time.

Kira crossed herself as I carried the ikon to her. She looked at it as though it were some creature that might suddenly spring to life in my hands, destroying what had become the only triumph she would ever know.

Kira. The Russian voice on the phone to Breton, and, an ancient ritual unraveling, and only one knew how it had to end.

"Take it," she said.

"It doesn't belong to me."

"Then give it away. I have what I want." She looked at Jamie. "So do you." Tentatively, she touched the ikon, running a finger down the edge. "His great victory," she said. "He knew about Nicholas, his father, what he'd done. It didn't matter. With the money they were going to change the world. Take it and go. Please."

She walked toward her husband and knelt down beside him, separated by the circle of candles. She bowed her head in prayer.

Outside, Jones was standing next to Conshocken, holding him up against the car. Jamie and I walked toward them.

"I'll kill you, Hunter," Conshocken said. "I'll find you and kill you."

"Can he do that?"

"Ed's a real patriot," Jones said. "A genuine go-getter."

"You're finished," Conshocken screamed at him.

The agent nodded like a waiter taking an order. "Hell, Ed," he said, smiling coldly, "I haven't even started with you yet."

Boris rolled down the window of the car and leaned his head out. "Hunter," he called and I walked over.

"Please," he said, "I would like to see it."

I held up the ikon.

The agent pushed Conshocken toward the passenger door.

"I think this is good-bye, Hunter," Boris said.

"Looks like it," I said and stuck out my hand. Boris took it and smiled.

"Take care of yourself, my friend. I will send you a postcard. Honest."

"You are such a liar, Boris."

We watched the car pull away, and I thought I saw Boris waving to us from the back window. Jamie and I started down the long drive. Jamie was nearly exhausted, and she held on to me as we walked. We were at the first turn when I heard a door slam shut behind us. I stopped and listened.

"Wait here," I said. She nodded and leaned against the rocks. I ran back toward the house, stopping beside the gate, almost afraid to go any farther. Peering through the snow, I saw a shadowy figure moving toward the birches at a slow deliberate march; a prisoner's pace. I nearly called out. Even now, I'm not sure why I didn't. Instead, I turned around and walked back down the road.

"What happened?" Jamie asked.

"Nothing," I said.

We were halfway down the mountain when the shot came. The sound echoed briefly, each echo growing fainter and fainter. Jamie stopped and looked up toward Zemlya. Her face was hidden in the darkness. I thought I heard her cry out softly. Then without saying a word, she took my hand and we walked down the mountain.

18

THAT NIGHT, at home, events sought their own level. The ikons sat against the far wall of the living room like unwanted guests who didn't know when to leave. Every time I turned around to get something, they were there. I built a fire and lay down on the floor and watched it burn. Jules lay down next to me, flopping heavily against my leg.

Jamie had gone upstairs to get ready for bed. When she came down, she was wearing her long blue flannel nightgown, hair combed over her shoulders.

I poked at the fire. Jules made room for Jamie.

"My dog finally learned some manners," I said. Jules put her head between her paws and was quiet.

Jamie laid her head on my lap and threw her legs over Jules' back. Jules yawned. It was a curiously comfortable configuration.

"Are we home, Hunter?" Jamie asked.

"Home and dry." She threw her arms around me, kissed my stomach and hugged me. I looked over my shoulder at the ikons stacked against the wall. Their black faces caught the light and sent it dancing over the floor-boards.

"What are you going to do with them?"

"Take them to Breton," I said.

"Do it soon," Jamie said.

She was building up to something. Deep in the fire, a spit of resin snapped.

"Kira told me you were in trouble this morning," she said.

"Did she tell you where I was?"

"It was a secret, remember?"

"It wasn't a secret, Jamie."

"Chernetzsky came to my house," she said. "He helped

me with my coat." Her voice grew sadder as she talked. "They put me in one of those rooms upstairs. Kira was the only one who talked to me. She came up with some food in the afternoon."

"Was Kharkovnakov there?"

"I didn't see him until after dark. Kira finally let me out and told me about Nicholas and the ikons. I saw Kharkovnakov then. He was so alone, Hunter."

"Where was Nicholas?"

"I don't know. They just disappeared, everyone. I heard a shot outside. After that, I blocked everything out. I didn't want to hear any more."

"Didn't Kira try to find you?"

"No," Jamie said, "only you."

As we went up to bed, Jamie stopped and looked at the ikons. She stood back from them, a fearful look on her face.

"I don't like them in the house," she said. "They frighten me."

"They won't hurt anything," I said.

"Won't they?" she said and started up the stairs. I bent down and stared into those eyes again.

"Please, Hunter," Jamie said. "Get them out of here."

"Soon," I said.

I wasn't completely certain I could promise that.

We returned to our routines. Jamie went to work. I stayed home and drifted through the house. I moved the ikons out of the living room and put them in the spare closet behind the kitchen. Something made me hold on to them.

Events sought their own level; a quick spiral to ground.

A few days later, she asked, "Where are they, Hunter?"

We were sitting at the kitchen table. I didn't say anything, pretending I hadn't heard her.

"Hunter," she said.

"What?"

"Just tell me where they are."

"They're in a closet."

"Then get rid of them. I don't care how you do it, but get rid of them."

168

"Tomorrow," I said. She stood up, shoving her chair back hard.

"Why are you still keeping them here?" she asked, her hand slapping out each word on the table.

"I don't understand it, either," I said, half smiling. "They don't want to leave."

Jamie went for her coat.

"I'm not coming back until they're gone."

"Tomorrow," I said. "Promise."

"I want them out of our life," she yelled and slammed the door.

"Tomorrow," I repeated to an empty room.

A few more days passed.

One morning Jules lay sleeping, her huge legs shivering. She made dream sounds in her throat. When I tried to pet her, she woke with a start and snapped at my hand. Everything seemed to be falling apart. I called Breton and told him I had some work for him to do.

Late in the afternoon, I saw them wheeling across the yard through the snow as they made their way to our door. Jamie walked beside the wheelchair, pointing at the house and laughing. I opened the door and a cold stream of air swept into the room as Jamie came through first, followed by Arnold Haddonford and Conrad. Jules wandered over to look at the new people.

"That's a very large animal," Arnold said. "I'll assume that he's harmless."

"She is," I said.

Jamie came over and gave me a perfunctory hug and a kiss on the cheek. "Hello, Hunter," she said, eyeing me suspiciously.

"How are you, Arnold?" I asked.

"I'm fine," he said. "How are you?" He raised any eyebrow and waited for my answer. When he didn't get one right away, he said, "Jamie tells me you two have had a pretty rough time of it."

"We're mending," I said. Jamie looked at me as if she didn't believe a word I said.

Arnold smiled. "I'm delighted to hear that." He looked into the living room. "You have an interesting home, Hunter."

169

"It grows on you," I said. Conrad was still standing awkwardly by the door. "How are you, Conrad?"

"I'm fine," he said.

"Good. Come in and sit down. You make me nervous when you stand at attention." Naturally, Conrad didn't move.

"Oh, for God's sake, Conrad, do something with yourself," Arnold said.

"Would anybody like some hot chocolate?" Jamie asked. "It won't take long to make it."

Arnold grinned. "I haven't had real hot chocolate since I was a boy. I'd love some."

"Conrad?"

"Yes, please," Conrad said. "I like your house very much."

"It does grow on you," Jamie said to him and went to the refrigerator for the milk. I think Conrad was a little taken with her. I couldn't blame him. So was I.

"Would you like to help, Conrad?" Jamie asked, and he stepped gratefully into the sanctuary of the kitchen.

I went over to the stove and started poking the fire. Arnold came over to where I was kneeling. He was wearing a blue blazer and an ascot, and Conrad had wrapped him up in a bright Scotch-plaid blanket. If it was possible, his face seemed pinker than usual. The cold air must have had a rejuvenating effect on him. He held his hands in front of the open door, warming them.

"I hadn't realized you were quite so self-sufficient, Hunter," Arnold said.

"A wood stove doesn't make me a pioneer."

"I wasn't referring to the stove," he said. "I had an interesting call from a friend of mine in Washington. You're making a name for yourself down there." He stopped to think about that. "I'm not certain that's a good thing," he said at last.

"Probably not," I said. "I got lucky."

"That as well," he said. He seemed mesmerized by the fire and stared empty-eyed into it. "I haven't seen your story in the *Times*. Did I miss it?"

"Nope, I just wrote it." I'd sent Rodger the story a week before. It had disappeared immediately into the great editorial maw at the magazine. Rodger had actually been decent enough to call and say that it was the best thing I'd ever done. I asked him when I'd see my money. Soon, he said. That was a promise, he said. I was back to eating metaphors again.

"So how's Martin Angle these days?" I asked.

Arnold grinned, and I grinned right along with him.

"He's left the country. It seems someone sent some interesting information to the right people and several layers of protection were quietly removed. He now resides in Costa Rica with the other fiduciary thugs. The tax people moved in as they always do whenever they sniff blood and they're now waiting for him to come home. If he ever does."

Jamie brought the hot chocolate over to the couch on a tray. Conrad followed behind her, at a loss for something else to do. I suggested he sit down and enjoy himself. That only seemed to confuse him. Arnold wheeled over next to the couch, and Jamie placed a cup in his hands. He took several sips and nodded approvingly. "It's very good, Jamie."

"Thank you," she said. "You should come here more often."

"Be careful," he said. "I'll take you at your word."

Conrad asked if he could put another log on the fire and I told him to go ahead. He got down in front of the stove and started poking around. Jules waddled over and lay down next to him. He reached over and scratched behind her ears. I looked at Arnold. He was staring at his cup, turning it around in his hands.

"I went to Kimberly's funeral," he said.

"How was it?"

"Like all funerals," he said. "Sad, a little unreal."

"Do you want to know what happened?"

"No," he said, "I already do."

Jamie gave Arnold a hard stare and asked Conrad if he wouldn't like to see the rest of the house. Conrad looked as if he'd been hit with a cattle prod. He was halfway to the stairs before Jamie moved off the couch.

When they were safely upstairs, Arnold asked, "Are you sure you're all right, Hunter?"

"You know I am, Arnold."

"I told her that when she called, of course," he said, a little embarrassed, "but she wanted me to take a look. I couldn't say no. I hope you don't mind."

"No," I said, and laughed. "I figured you'd want to take a good look at them yourself before I gave them back to the professor."

Arnold lowered his head and then looked up, grinning. "If it isn't too much trouble," he said.

I got them out of the closet near the kitchen and set them up in front of Arnold. Haddonford drew in a quick breath.

"My God," he said and wheeled directly in front of them. "They're absolutely stunning."

From the top of the stairs, Jamie said, "You're supposed to tell him to get rid of them, Arnold, not swoon over them like some schoolboy." Arnold made an apologetic gesture. "Look at you," she said, coming down the stairs. "Look at both of you."

I managed to stop her at the bottom of the stairs.

"Jamie," I said, "I'm taking them to Breton's tomorrow." I held up my hand.

"Is that the truth, Hunter?" she asked.

"Honest," I said, holding up both hands.

Breton's house was a mess, but it looked as if he'd made a last-minute stab at visual order. The garbage was piled in the corner of the kitchen according to its generic classification. One half of the sink was filled with dishes and dirty water. A thin scum of orange fat floated amid the cups and plates. The driveway had not been shoveled, and his car was covered with snow.

He opened the back door dressed in the same sweater and pants he had been wearing when I first met him. He had even shaved—or had tried to. His eyes dropped to the ikons. He took one and asked me inside. We carried the ikons to his study.

The study was a mess. Several cups, some half filled with cold tea, sat on the table next to his chair. He had cleaned up his desk; the acid had left a grainy white scar on the top.

"I'm sorry for the way things are," he said. "It's been hard for me."

"Have you seen Vera?"

Breton flinched. "Yesterday," he said. "She's still in intensive care. I think she recognized me." The memory seemed to embarrass him. He smiled awkwardly and fingered the ikons.

"Do you know which one came from the church?" he asked.

"Yes," I said and pointed to it. Nicholas must have given the original to Kharkovnakov, one more link between them. I was sure Angle never knew. I was just as certain that Boris did.

"I want you to clean them."

Breton picked up the church ikon and took it to the desk. He laid it over the stain and turned on the light, studying the cracks across the face, the minute shattering of centuries. He was wide-eyed with excitement.

"Help me carry them to the basement," he said.

We laid them on the workbench, side by side.

"They're exquisite," Breton said. He ran his hand along the edge, caressing the wood. "If one of them is a fake, then it's extremely well done."

"Maybe they're both real," I said. "How long will it take you?"

"For a simple authentication? An hour, less perhaps."

"I want to see the faces."

Breton examined the ikons again.

"Come back tonight. Six o'clock," he said and began cutting a piece of flannel.

Breton was waiting nervously when Jamie and I got there at quarter to six. He led us into the basement without saying very much. The ikons were set up on two easels in front of the workbench, covered with pieces of flannel.

"It wasn't what I expected," he said.

"I want to get this over with," Jamie said.

Breton took the flannel off one of the ikons. It was another "Christ Painted Without Hands."

"This is the fake," Breton said. "If that's what you want to call it."

He had cleaned only the face, leaving the rest of the ikon dark, impenetrable.

"Not as common as most," he went on, "but not a masterpiece by any means. I'd say from the early to late seventeenth century. The craftsmanship is very good. It's been altered recently by someone who knew a great deal about ikons. There are probably only one or two people in this country who could tell if it had been worked on at all."

He put his hand on the second ikon.

"This one," he said, "I simply don't know. It *is* real. Thirteenth-century, I know that much."

He pulled the flannel off the ikon.

It wasn't Christ. The face on the ikon belonged to a man of indeterminate age, hair hanging in broken braids alongside his sunken cheeks. His forehead was covered with cuts, each wound colored in bright red. It looked as if they were still bleeding.

"Fyodor," I said.

"A self-portrait," Breton said. He touched the face. "Look at the eyes," he whispered.

The eyes held me. Vivid black ovals on pale yellowish skin, they stared past me as though they were gazing into some great distance.

I didn't have to look any more. Jamie pulled on my arm, taking me away. "Let's go home, Hunter," she said, and we walked up the stairs with Breton behind us.

A car was parked behind Breton's in the driveway. Two men sat in the front seat with the engine running, parking lights on. I recognized them immediately. Breton peered over Jamie's shoulder and shouted at them. "You can't park here. This is private property."

"I don't think they can hear you," Jamie said.

Breton stepped between us. "Whether they can hear me or not," he said, "they should know better."

Samuels rolled down his window on the passengers side. Breton approached the window, talking all the while, his voice filled with indignation. The other agent leaned over from his side and held up something for him to see. Breton stopped talking. The other agent spoke firmly and rapidly. Breton came back to the house.

"They're from the government," he said, dazed. "They said they're going to take the ikons. They can't do that,

174

can they? Without a warrant or anything? Just walk in and take something that doesn't belong to them?"

The two agents got out of the car and stood by the doors, waiting.

"They can do anything they want," I said, watching them.

"Hello, Hunter," Jones said. "Long time no see."

"Going into business for yourself?"

"Nah," he said, "this is official." He pulled out his wallet. I looked at the card.

"Your name really is Jones," I said.

"Nobody believes me when I tell them."

"I wonder why. How's Ed?"

"Ed who?"

"Nobody important," I said. "I don't suppose you found out anything about a guy named Boris."

"Never heard of him," he said, taking a small photograph out of his coat pocket. It was Boris standing in front of the Grand Canyon. He was wearing a big white cowboy hat and a sleazy smile. He looked like the happiest man in the whole goddam world.

"Okay?" Jones asked and put the picture back in his pocket. "Now where is it?"

"Downstairs," I said. Jones started for the basement. "Let me help you," I said.

In the basement, Jones looked at both of the ikons and shook his head. He pointed at the Fyodor.

"That guy looks like he belongs in a zoo," he said, turning toward me. "So, which one is it?"

I pointed to the fake. "That one. The other one was somebody's idea of a joke."

"You want a joke," Jones said, picking up the fake, "you should talk to Ed these days."

"Ed who?" I said.

"Never heard of him," Jones said and walked up the stairs with the ikon.